PETROLEUM TRANSFER ENGINEER

RICHARD KLIN

Published by Underground Voices
www.undergroundvoices.com
Editor contact: Cetywa Powell

ISBN #: 978-0-9988923-3-7
Printed in the United States of America.

To Lily

Petroleum Transfer Engineer

PART 1

1.

Eleven at night was when he began to work: the graveyard shift, which would last until seven in the morning. The gas station, even at this later hour, was still extraordinarily busy, with cars streaming in from the Expressway and crowding into the brightly-lit lanes. The summer heat continued to be a factor, the asphalt and concrete warm after a full day of sun, the station made hotter yet by the exhaust fumes and the odor of gasoline, the mammoth lights illuminating all the activity.

Tillman's Gulf was a huge endeavor, with an entire side of the station designated for Philadelphia-bound traffic and another side for traffic heading in the direction of Atlantic City. At eleven it was the Philly section that was the most hectic, with people returning home from their time at the shore, the beaches, the Atlantic City casinos. Traffic, though, had not fully abated on the other side. Drivers—lots of them—still proceeded in the direction of Atlantic City, Ocean City, Wildwood, Cape May.

He pumped gas, took money, made change, gave directions. Because it was so intensely crowded, there was an unspoken understanding that now was not really the time to ask the attendant to check the oil or wash the windows. Those things were more the domain of the day shift, when washing windows was expected as a matter of course, when checking oil and sometimes transmission fluid was part of the routine. And sometimes Mr. Tillman himself was on the premises during the day, which meant that the garbage cans had to be emptied out or the shithouses cleaned.

Many of these nighttime customers felt compelled, for some reason, to share their experiences with Francis as he pumped their gas. He was forced to listen to endless summations of their time at the shore or—even more uninteresting—their experiences at the casinos: They couldn't find any ten-dollar blackjack tables. Or they found the ten-dollar blackjack tables. They did really well.

Or just the opposite: They gave it all back to the casinos. They saw Don Rickles at the Golden Nugget, Steve and Eydie at Harrah's. They had a great time, they got sunburned, they needed directions, they needed food. They had to go to the bathroom.

Inexplicably, nighttime was when the customers lost their bearings, having no idea where they were, no clue whatsoever as to how to get back to New York or Pennsylvania or Ohio, assuming that anyone who pumped gas here possessed a special, intuitive aptitude for directions and was thoroughly conversant with the intricacies of turnpikes, parkways, thruways.

Francis, on a regular basis, was also peppered with steady requests for information on where to stay, where to eat. But being from the area rendered him, paradoxically, completely at a loss to recommend anything: Obviously, he had never stayed here as a tourist. His own dining preferences tilted toward the Dairy Queen near the bay or Casa Enzo's subs, neither of which would pass muster with vacationers. His fail-safe solution was, no matter what, to automatically direct travelers to the Dover Hotel in Ocean City, the giant pink structure that loomed over the beach. Who, he reasoned, wouldn't like the Dover?

Where's the closest place to get something to eat? was another question Francis heard with near-constant regularity, and he was forced to point out—again and again, as patiently as possible—the Garden House, which was right next door. This particular query, for some reason, outraged Dewey, the shift manager. Dewey was an imposing figure who towered over the pumps, with thick, combed-back black hair and huge glasses that eerily reflected the lights of the station and the cars. "Fuck 'em," he would insist vehemently, "if they're too goddamn stupid to see that it's *right next* door."

Eleven until seven made for a very long night. As the hours progressed, there were lulls, opportunities to run next door to the Garden House for a soda or chips or their rotgut coffee. Francis "couldn't" help but notice, in the course of these visits, the same two cashiers. One had shortish hair and glasses. It seemed to Francis that this particular cashier was slightly confused by her job duties, perhaps intimidated by some of the more rough-and-tumble clientele, ill at ease with the steady trickle of state troopers who made their appearance. Francis had once glimpsed this cashier exiting her little car, self-consciously adjusting her synthetic brown Garden House uniform. Emblazoned on her back window—like a beacon—was a Haverford College sticker. Since then he had felt an almost desperate impulse to inform this cashier with the shortish hair, glasses, and Haverford sticker on her back window, that he too was a college student. Or, if she was a stickler for technicalities, he would inform her that he *had been* a college student, now in temporary exile at Tillman's Gulf. He racked his brain for a subtle, yet effective way of communicating all this to the Haverford girl. In dramatic contrast to the rest of the gas-station crew, here was a real-life English major, a regular presence at Enoch Place, the department's stately headquarters. Enoch Place was where he had dazzled one and all with his artful extrapolation of Sinclair Lewis's *Babbitt*, linking the novel's eponymous protagonist to the worldview and platitudes of Ronald Reagan. Perhaps this Garden House cashier who also attended Haverford College would be astonished to discover him, a diamond in the rough. Amid the base commerce of a mediocre fast-food tourist trap and a gas station situated off the Atlantic City Expressway, she would find a kindred spirit.

But almost exactly as Francis seriously began to contemplate truly striking up a conversation with her, pinpricks of doubt began to assail him. There was a growing awareness that he was garbed in a fluorescent orange shirt, a blue Gulf patch presenting itself right above the shirt pocket. His right hand was calloused and raw from hours upon hours at the gas pump. His arms, his face, were smudged. He smelled of unleaded regular.

The other cashier seemed a little older and a polar opposite to the Haverford student. This cashier made a point of joking around with the customers, often laughing uproariously. She had, Francis gleaned, grown up right around here, in Engelston, and knew some of the troopers by name. He imagined she had quit school at sixteen, living a life of adventure and continuous sex; wise in the ways of the world that he probably couldn't even begin to comprehend. But almost exactly as Francis seriously began to contemplate truly striking up a conversation with *her*, pinpricks of doubt—of an entirely different nature—began to assail him. Now he was a bookish college boy, a marshmallow. She certainly knew more about cars than he did—which wasn't too difficult, as he knew next to nothing. The orange Gulf shirt and smudges, even the calloused right hand, were pathetic attempts to cover up what he really was. The tough Engelston girl would see right through him: Who the fuck was he trying to fool with his Gulf uniform?

Consequently, he spoke to neither cashier.

2.

Cliff worked at the station until two in the morning; incredibly easy to have around, hippie-like in appearance, with longish blond hair and wire-rimmed glasses. He was attending Bible school near Hammonton with the aspiration to become an evangelist. Improbably, he had spent some time in the Marines, which seemed impossible to imagine. As a teenager, Cliff had lost himself in the world of marijuana and alcohol abuse, going so far as to once swap pot for fuel at a gas station near his home. Now, though, he was a Christian, responsive to the word of God, and eager to share the good news with the world.

The customers, as a general rule, were required to turn off their engines when gas was being dispensed, but a good deal of the time they needed to be reminded of this. It seemed counterintuitive to keep one's engine running when gas was being pumped, yet Francis had to remind the customers over and over again, molding his *Please turn off your engine* into a calm—yet authoritative—utterance. There were occasions when it got so massively busy that he simply couldn't be bothered to invoke his standard *Please turn off your engine*. Cliff, though, was an admirable stickler, unwavering in the turn-off-your-engine rule no matter how busy or hectic the station got.

With Dewey floating back and forth between the two sides, Francis and Cliff could handle the traffic flow, although the pace could be frenetic, with Francis functioning akin to a skilled short-order cook, servicing two cars at the same time, and, when required, taking credit-card payments: speedily jotting down the license-plate information, rapidly running the card through the little contraption right by the pumps, adroitly seizing the slider and pulling it in a quick, emphatic motion as the transaction became official, and then briskly handing everything over to the customer to sign.

In the midst of all this crush, there would occasionally be a car that absolutely, positively needed its oil checked, and Francis could handle that as well, although there was always a brief moment of trepidation when he needed to instantaneously ascertain how to open the hood and just as instantaneously find the dipstick. The rest was relatively easy, as he was able to dash over to the shed, grab a can of oil, open it, and dispense it into the car as quickly as possible, all the while taking the greatest of care to ensure the oil didn't drip or spill.

It had been during one of his first few weeks—the afternoon shift—when a car had pulled in, a female driver at the helm. Her husband, curiously, was sprawled out in the backseat, dead to the world. The car had needed a quart of oil, which Francis duly poured, but some of the oil had dripped into the hot interior. He looked down to see dancing orange flames. It took a solid moment for his brain to register what he was actually viewing. "The car's on fire," he announced loudly, almost in puzzlement, and the driver, in understandable hysterics, bolted out. "The car's on fire," she shrieked to her husband, who remained oblivious, lying prone. "Honey, the car's on fire," she screamed again as her husband finally roused himself from his stupor.

Norm—the occasional fill-in—was also working the afternoon shift and he grabbed the fire extinguisher. Norm had served in Vietnam and Francis assumed he'd be adept in using an extinguisher, but Norm examined it for a moment and then asked Francis if *he* knew how to use it, which, of course, he didn't. So Francis and Norm stared at each other while the woman continued to scream. The husband stirred, muttering something unintelligible, and it fell to Dutch, who had owned his own Sunoco station on Creslea Road for years and years, to commandeer the extinguisher and put a stop to the fire. Fortunately, the car, its inhabitants, and all of the Tillman's crew were unscathed. Later, it was Joe—Norm's friend and fellow Vietnam vet—

who hung the *Francis's Fire Station* sign on one of the shack windows.

To keep from being utterly and completely consumed by boredom, Francis kept a mental tally of the array of license plates that passed through the station. There was no rhyme or reason. One week favored Massachusetts and Florida, another week was heavy with Michigan. South Carolina and Kansas, he concluded, had the most attractive license plates, Ohio the least. California had the strangest letter-number combination. He set a lofty goal for himself: to see an Alaska and Hawaii.

He also kept an informal count of the various forms of address that the customers offered up. To be called *sir* was gratifying indeed, but this rarely happened. Instead, he was hailed with the appellations *bro, cap'n, boss, bruss,* and *chief,* all of which were bandied about at regular intervals.

A pink Cadillac came through the station. So did limos. Sports cars. Trucks. Buses. Motorcycles. Convertibles.

A boxer. A priest. A van full of Hare Krishnas, leaving behind some colorful literature depicting flying elephants and women with a multitude of arms. This provoked a rare burst of ill humor on the part of the even-tempered Cliff, who declared there was nothing whatsoever of merit to be found in this sort of thing and disgustedly crumpled it all up into a ball, dropping it emphatically into one of the garbage cans.

The weather guy from channel 19. Chinese people. The airport shuttle van from Philly, driven by the same grizzled man with the astonishingly obvious toupee that resembled swirls of ice cream. A stunningly clueless family, bound for vacation in Ocean City, Maryland; Francis had to break the news to them that they were, in actuality, en route to Ocean City, New Jersey.

Some drivers couldn't pay at all, their money lost to the casinos, and in desperation they would offer six-packs or liquor in lieu of payment, a spare tire, fishing gear. The policy was to give these customers a few dollars' worth of fuel, gratis, getting them out of the station and on their way. Mr. Tillman extracted his pound of flesh by having the employees write down the offending car's license-plate number, which was then added to a list taped on the side of the shed for all to see, the words *Sad Story* emblazoned in thick, accusatory black ink.

A busload of Playboy bunnies, en route to god-knows-what sort of event, had also graced Tillman's Gulf. They were shockingly coarse, hanging out of the open windows and screaming things like *I've got the biggest tits!* and incorporating gas-station terminology like *hose* and *pump* in various unimaginative obscenities. Even gas-station lifers like Dutch and Sonny, the day-shift manager, seemed appalled. To Francis's surprise, Vince, the newest employee, was unmoved by these Playboy bunnies. Vince was fresh from the navy and inclined toward constantly scratching his balls. He regaled his coworkers with tales of blanket parties, in which sailors took their blankets, wrapped a bar of soap in a tight coil, and then proceeded to beat the living shit out of some poor, unfortunate motherfucker. Francis had assumed—incorrectly, as it turned out—that Vince would be enthralled by these foul-mouthed bunnies with their big tits and innuendo.

3

He told himself, at regular intervals, that college was fading fast. It was a concept fraught with complexity. In some ways college wasn't fading fast at all. Much of it felt ongoing, like a portal into a parallel universe: He was still among the mass of students streaming down University Avenue, or he was back amid the pulsating music of the Harmony Lounge.

His books remained stacked in a large pile in a corner of his bedroom: *Movie-Made America* and *Pale Fire* and *Go Down, Moses*. From time to time he would creep over to this stack of books and actually stare, too afraid to crack them open, as if he would be introducing some hidden toxicity into their pure, unsullied pages. And then this trepidation would be replaced by a wave of disgust so intense that it was, at times, physically palpable, requiring that he sit down on the floor.

Those inane, endless discussions of Hemingway's short stories or the ramifications of the Falklands conflict, all of which seemed so important at the time, so pathetically important. The special April Fools' edition of the school newspaper that everyone—including him—found so vastly amusing. And then, as he sat on his bedroom floor, a cascade of shame rained down on him as he recalled the missed classes, the incremental lack of studying, the sleeping late. The requisite meeting with Dr. Hanson to discuss term-paper topics, only to discover that the format had changed weeks before. It was nakedly obvious that Francis hadn't attended class all semester. He remembered it as being one of the most humiliating moments of his life.

He'd become consumed by the TV-trivia video game at Dough-Re-Mi, the pizza and sub shop right off Imre Nagy Park. Here, finally, was something he could excel at. It became a daily part of his schedule. A basket of garlic knots and can of Dr Pepper by his side, he eventually branched out into movie trivia and then even geography trivia, gaining increased proficiency as he went along, steadily setting scoring records in a variety of categories. The champion was accorded the privilege of entering his name, which showed up on a display of the top-ten winners' circle. In time, he began to occupy so many of these slots that it became necessary to employ an array of clever pseudonyms—*Beelzebub, Old Scratch, Torquemada*. How droll, that he had come up with those names.

If only he had left college because of unrelenting partying or debauchery. It had been just the opposite. He had simply faded away, his life as a student evaporating into a fog of TV trivia and garlic knots.

And then, of course, his thoughts drifted to Annie, as they often did. Those thoughts came in the form of random vignettes. The time when he spotted her at the bookstore. That long, long lunch at the Selden Tavern—the turning point, really—where she'd looked about as vulnerable as he'd ever seen her, both of them commandeering a table amid the venerable dark paneling, the display of antique trains, the mountain of bleu cheese on their salads.

One night at the Harmony. The music, as usual, was thundering and they'd run into that oddball Norwegian student who'd attached herself to them for the entire evening. And he and Annie didn't mind; not really, except that they both couldn't remember the name of this oddball Norwegian, and even at the end of a long night together at the Harmony they were never able to ascertain what her name was. And then they would run into her quite often, on University Avenue or in the library, and she would call out, with accented gusto: "Francis! Annie!" And they never knew what to call her.

At times the memories would proceed with such intensity that he was transported to somewhere else entirely. It was raining, the fat patter of drops beating out a rhythm on the roof of Annie's tiny off-campus apartment, the two of them in bed, dozing off for hours and hours and hours. It had seemed like the apex of his entire existence.

He imagined that she had utterly and completely forgotten about him, all traces of his existence obliterated, wiped from her memory.

4.

Francis's mother and father couldn't have been happier to have him back home, as if college had been some sort of painful aberration and now, here, his future was about to triumphantly unfold. His mother, with great avidity, regularly perused the want ads in the Sunday *Journal-Bulletin*, bubbling over with exaggerated enthusiasm. A new restaurant in Haslams Landing needed a manager. There were job agencies that specialized in placement. Or perhaps he should explore the possibilities at the casinos. Atlantic City was full of potential.

His father was a fount of expansive, ambitious plans. Francis could enroll at the community college, develop a foundation in economics, which was essential. "You're right where you should be," his mother gushed, which made him feel decidedly worse. He was, after all, pumping gas at Tillman's Gulf. This was not where he should be at all. But then, exactly, where was he *supposed* to be? Nobody knew.

There was one tangible benefit in being a defrocked college student. His parents had decided, now that he was a wage-earner, that he needed his own car. Accordingly, Francis came into possession of a flimsy little blue Chevette. It had no pickup whatsoever, but it was his; his very own car.

Mr. Tillman supplied the bright-orange Gulf shirts. Additionally, he provided the money for Francis to purchase three regulation-blue work pants, available at the army-navy store in Absecon. This astonished his parents, who felt it was an unprecedented act of generosity for a businessman to actually supply work pants. Mr. Tillman also provided free passes for the Expressway toll, issuing Francis an official-looking booklet with a month's worth of tear-out tickets. This was another example of Mr. Tillman's supreme generosity and brought out paroxysms of joy from his parents. Francis couldn't shake the sense that these exaggerated hosannas to Mr. Tillman were to assuage their lurking fear that he would quit this job at the Gulf station and make yet another of his many horrible decisions.

To make matters more uncomfortable, Jeanette, his older sister, had not only graduated from college but had landed a plum job at radio station FM 96—the Rockin' Wave. The Rockin' Wave had recently relocated from Atlantic City to right here in Leedsville, in a brand-new office building constructed next to the HappyMart on Wabash Road, where he and all the rest of the kids had biked to on a regular basis, quarter in hand. And much later, of course, it was where one went to purchase rolling paper.

The Rockin' Wave's relocation had engendered a good deal of attention. Leedsville's only real business facility—not counting the rowdy, grimy bars that lined Bay Street on the other side of town in the section known as the Point—had been the insurance company. Now there was a radio station.

Much of Jeanette's job duties involved writing ad copy, a crucial first step, as she'd explained when she held court at the dinner table—which was often—in this, her first important job out of college. And of course Francis was genuinely happy for her, his supremely capable older sibling. But there was something bizarre in this transformation: The straight-A student and passionate force in Leedsville High's Latin Club who'd been only nominally captivated by radio fare, now discussing ad revenue, demographics, playlists; Francis sitting slack-jawed as Jeanette discussed FM 96's upcoming Big Kahuna Weekend, featuring DJ appearances and giveaways. Their father nodded his head sagaciously—as if owning the same store for a good twenty years granted him an intrinsic understanding of the ins and outs of running a radio station; a special insight into the process of assembling a Big Kahuna Weekend.

Management, in a perpetual quest to redefine FM 96's reach, had engaged in a long, protracted debate on the advisability of changing its tagline from the Rockin' Wave to, instead, Rock of Ages. The station had split into two camps: those who favored Rock of Ages and those were opposed. Jeanette's faction had felt strongly that the inadvertently religious connotations of Rock of Ages could confuse their target demographic. And so, for now, Rockin' Wave held sway.

Francis did enjoy the novelty of hearing her ideas actually make it onto the air. She had spent an enormous amount of time and effort crafting the appropriate ad for Kicks, a raucous new bar down in Wildwood. Jeanette, who had probably never even entered a sweaty, ear-splitting bar in her entire life, had nevertheless hatched a bona fide, authentic ad that one could hear on FM 96 at regular intervals: a deep voice booming out the words *Kicks kicks in the rock and roll!* while some godawful local band wailed away in the background.

5.

There was something interesting and distinctive, to be sure, in wearing a uniform for the first time in his life, driving off to work clad in his bright-orange Gulf shirt, regulation-blue work pants, newly purchased work boots. Francis had no need, now, to cough up money in order to travel via the Atlantic City Expressway. His new status as a Tillman's employee enabled him to hand his pass to the toll collector. He was now part of the Expressway elite, privileged to travel for free.

It was Mr. Tillman's voice that was the single most memorable thing about him, a deep, rumbling wheeze with foghorn-like attributes. On Francis's very first day of work, Mr. Tillman sat him down in the front office and commenced with a painfully detailed recitation of the intricacies of working here at the station, Francis doing his best to listen attentively. Soon, though, the first twinges of embarrassment began to prickle, which only grew more pronounced as Mr. Tillman's monologue stretched on and on. Meanwhile, the gas station was consumed by frenetic motion—employees scurrying back and forth, entering and exiting the bare-bones office, and Francis sitting in the midst of this. One large, somewhat scary-looking man in a rumpled Gulf uniform, heedless of the gas station's rapid-fire pace, lumbered along with a quiet authority, calmly working around the immovable force that was Mr. Tillman, gathering a sheath of papers, a roll of money, while Mr. Tillman continued his tutorial.

The orientation came to an end with an unexpected, almost avuncular reassurance that Francis needn't worry about having sufficient time to eat. The station did not utilize time cards; he could sit and eat a proper meal. "But don't—" Mr. Tillman began, and to Francis's surprise the creased, wrinkled face broke into a wide smile—"Don't set a place for yourself at the desk with candlelight and silverware!" And here Mr. Tillman broke into a loud, wheezy guffaw. Francis joined in, laughing along appreciatively.

At first he worked the very hot, extremely crowded day shift, which began at seven in the morning and concluded at three in the afternoon. The heat was occasionally broken by sudden, heavy downpours, the crew scuttling into the shed, all of them donning the hot, constricting yellow rain slickers.

He soon skipped around in a crazy quilt of shifts: six in the evening until two in the morning; the graveyard shift from eleven to seven; back to seven-to-three, three-to-eleven, six-to-two. His mother unfailingly packed him the same comforting meal each and every time: A sandwich. A bag of grapes. A chunk of sharp Wisconsin cheese wrapped in tinfoil. Cookies.

Tillman's Gulf was not, emphatically, a repair place. The idea was to provide gas, wash windows, check oil and transmission if requested, and send the drivers on their way. There were provisions in the event of the occasional emergency, with the shift manager undertaking a quick repair job in the back garage. Francis, luckily, could get by with his nonexistent knowledge of cars.

He did learn how to check oil, transmission fluid, how to utilize the credit-card machine. He discovered that the gas tank for Volkswagens was in the front of the car, not the back. He learned that there was a special, individual pump for diesel. He became reasonably adept at window-washing, at dispensing rudimentary directions, at regulating the flow of gasoline coming out of the pump.

It fell to him, more often than not, to clean out the bathrooms, which in essence meant replacing the paper towels in the dispenser, emptying out the garbage, and spraying massive amounts of industrial-grade disinfectant all over the sinks and toilet. Having to tackle the women's bathroom always brought on a measure of discomfiture, and he took to knocking loudly on the door over and over before cautiously proceeding inside. During his first attempt, he utterly botched filling the towel dispenser, spilling paper towels all over the floor and coming close to actually breaking the entire apparatus off the wall. He then cravenly assigned the blame to the previous occupants, a mother and her toddler girl.

These bathrooms at Tillman's Gulf were rarely, if ever, referred to as bathrooms. The standard appellation was *shithouse*, which Francis once sprang on his parents and Jeanette after dinner. The quick pace of the station did seem to prevent customers from lingering in the bathrooms and they were only sporadically utilized. But inwardly, Francis recoiled every time Mr. Tillman, in that rumbling timbre, issued the command: "Francis, go clean them shithouses." *Go clean them shithouses* seemed like some of the ugliest, most grating words in the English language.

There was no telling when this command would be uttered. It was as if Mr. Tillman had an internal sense of when them shithouses needed to be cleaned, and suddenly the words sprang forth, carrying over the gas pumps: *Francis, go clean them shithouses.*

After an entire shift spent pumping gas, regular soap was altogether useless. The crew at Tillman's Gulf utilized an ultra-abrasive, scorching powdered soap that cascaded out of the aged dispenser above the industrial, corroded sink in the far reaches of the station, back behind the repair bays. The powder scalded, burning off the gasoline and the oil and sweat and dirt. And then, these ablutions completed, Francis would sneak an astonished glance into the dingy, cracked mirror that hung precariously above the sink. And each and every time he glimpsed the reflection of a tired workingman, hair matted down with sweat, face lined with physical exhaustion, flecks of dirt and smudges. Was he to be horrified or intrigued by this metamorphosis? And what, he couldn't but help wonder, would Annie possibly make of this?

6.

That hulking man who had hovered nearby during Mr. Tillman's introductory monologue was Sonny, the day manager: a huge, lumbering presence; almost entirely bald, save for some unruly strands of yellowish hair. His arms were massive to the point that Francis imagined Sonny could knock over, if he so desired, one of the gas pumps. Sonny's tilted gait was as distinctive as Mr. Tillman's voice: so hunched over that he almost seemed to be lurching. The intimidation factor, though, faded relatively quickly as Sonny, to Francis's surprise, warmed up to him, called him "kid," and displayed some unexpected curiosity about his college life, his parents and sister. Within time, Sonny began to confide his misgivings about Mr. Tillman, taking Francis aside for a hurried, confidential spleen-venting. These sort of encounters soon became routine, with Sonny essentially uttering the same thing every time without significant deviation—almost word for word: "I've got nothing but respect for the man," he would begin over-earnestly. That disclaimer out of the way, he would move in for the kill: "But he just *don't know* what he's doing anymore."

And then there was a pause. "He's getting senile," Sonny would continue. And now his mien would quickly shift from thoughtful concern to growing contempt, the mouth twisting, preparing for the vehement conclusion: "He should just *stay the fuck home.*"

And then there would be another pause, leading up to the final summation: "It's fucked-up, kid." This came to be Sonny's constant refrain: *It's fucked-up, kid*, trotted out for a myriad of occasions—if it was too hot or if there was a sudden repair to be done or if Mr. Tillman was coming in for the afternoon. *It's fucked-up, kid.*

Dutch was a short, squat older man around Mr. Tillman's age, usually positioned—sentry-like—in the middle of the concrete walkway that separated the Atlantic

City–bound side from the Philly-bound, gazing out intently, as if expecting some sort of enemy incursion, cigarette packs firmly ensconced in his two shirt pockets. Dutch, for many years, had run his own Sunoco station at the far end of Creslea Road. For reasons Francis was not privy to, he had sold his business and subsequently went to work here at Tillman's Gulf. Dutch occupied a nebulous slot. Officially, he was part of the crew like all the others, but because of his age and previous history as a boss, he assumed an unofficial supervisory role, treated with deference—grudging deference, it seemed to Francis—by Sonny and Dewey.

At times, Mr. Tillman joined Dutch in his sentry duties, both perched together side by side in the middle of the walkway, like two not necessarily very wise old owls. Dutch seemed to detest everything: the hot weather, the limousines, slanty-eyed Puerto Ricans, and most of the customers. "Keep your eyes open out there," he would intone to Francis from time to time in his cigarette-inflected timbre, mostly in jest. It soon became as much of a tagline as Sonny's *It's fucked-up, kid.*

One Sunday morning, Francis, his parents, and Jeanette headed to Buzby's Pancake House. This was somewhat out of the ordinary. Sundays, for the most part, were for lazing around at home, perusing the fat *Journal-Bulletin*: the color comics, *Parade* magazine, extra features.

He had stopped at Buzby's a few times after his shifts at the gas station, enjoying the novelty of this new persona as a uniform-clad, smudged worker coming in for coffee and sustenance after exhausting physical labor. This Sunday morning, as expected, Buzby's was packed with families, old people; the heady odors of food and coffee augmenting the festive air that permeated the atmosphere. A cheerful older hostess, sprig of flowers tucked into her shirt, led them to their table. Francis, to his great joy, was able to indulge his newfound passion for Buzby's coconut pancakes. After the meal's conclusion, as they were getting up from their table, none other than Mr. Tillman himself suddenly materialized, garbed in a suit and tie and most certainly having come from church. Here, in this context, he was surprisingly courtly, informing the family that he had just entered, spotted them from across the room, and come over to say hello.

And as loathe as he was to admit something like this to himself, it was flattering. His parents, of course, were positively agog at Mr. Tillman's solicitude.

"He's the best boss you'll ever have," his father pronounced fervently. Additional praise for Mr. Tillman was subsequently trotted out at regular intervals by both his mother and father, in increasingly inflated terms: Mr. Tillman, the wise and judicious helmsman. The fact that Mr. Tillman eschewed a time clock was an admirable sign of leniency, all too rare in a business owner. The Tillman's pay rate, above minimum wage, was another shrewd, effective move, ensuring a level of professionalism and employee loyalty. His mother intimated that without Mr. Tillman's watchful eye the employees would steal him blind.

What undergirded this excessive praise was, of course, his parents' continuous effort to forestall the prospect of him quitting his job. Leaving college had been catastrophic enough. At least now, though, he was gainfully employed. Jeanette, in her well-meaning, blundering way, also got into the act. It had dawned on her that she worked in a station—a radio station—and Francis too worked in a station. A gas station, of course, was in no way comparable to a radio station, but Jeanette willfully obliterated these distinctions, interested in comparisons between these two varied stations, the similarities and differences in the spectrum of customer expectations and services offered. It was all patently absurd. He was being pitied, catered to as you would a mental incompetent. Yet it was hard to take real offense. Jeanette meant well.

All this effort on the part of his parents and sister was unnecessary. There was no reason to praise Mr. Tillman in such inflated, exalted terms; no reason to exhibit such respectful interest in the gas station's mode of operation. Francis was, for now, staying put. There was no other place to go.

7.

The denizens of the Barbarians motorcycle gang would occasionally swoop into the gas station; thirty or forty on their mammoth Harleys, descending en masse. Francis had vague memories of a long-ago incident in which a Barbarian had killed a bouncer at some rowdy bar in the township. There had been a brief, genuine police manhunt, just like on TV, and the Barbarian was quickly apprehended.

The customers seemed pained—often on the verge of outright fear—to unexpectedly be in the midst of a biker gang, but in these situations the Barbarians wanted gas, not mayhem. And yet, as quiet insurance, a watchful trooper car always materialized unobtrusively off to the side of the station. Francis never knew if Sonny or Dutch had put in a call or if the Barbarians were monitored as a matter of course.

To Francis's surprise, the Barbarians, viewed up close, were much older and scraggly-looking than he'd imagined. Their weathered, grimy jackets bore a series of memorials to the legion of fallen comrades: Things like *In Memory of Little Jeff* or *Gone But Not Forgotten* emblazoned on a huge gravesite, followed by a lengthy list of the dead. Each and every jacket featured the incorrectly punctuated *Barbarian's*. The proper use of an apostrophe, apparently, was not a high priority in Barbarian circles. And Francis had to laugh at himself for even noticing. He imagined himself approaching the bikers and urging them to cleave to the accepted strictures of the English language and shed that errant apostrophe.

The Barbarians were not even remotely threatening. "Never any trouble at all," Joe would say. He was consistently one of the nicest Tillman's employee: cheerful, even-keeled. He seemed perpetually fascinated by the elaborate, formidable Harleys, approaching the bikers with open admiration, venturing forth with a knowledgeable comment or informed query. The affable Joe had not only been in Vietnam, Francis came to discover, but it had been his particular duty to collect the bodies of the dead. Joe had related all this with his typical cheery nonchalance and supplied no further details. The oil companies, he had asserted to Francis, had cut a deal with the North Vietnamese. They were permitted, in the thick of the fighting, to drill with impunity. He had seen it himself.

One late night, when it had been raining off and on, a Barbarian van pulled in. Francis was mildly surprised at the appearance of a van, assuming the Barbarians only traveled about exclusively on Harleys, not vans. He put the nozzle into the tank to, as instructed, fill 'er up, when suddenly he heard some voices, laughter. There was movement in the back of the van; a few smiling girls' faces suddenly popped up in the back window and then disappeared just as quickly. He heard some more laughing, some talking. The Barbarians were bringing along their old ladies, apparently—or whatever their terminology was. Before he had time to process this, the tall, bearded Barbarian driver got out of the van and strolled over to where Francis was.

He groaned inwardly. Some customers could get persnickety about gasoline spilling out onto their precious vehicles. He assumed this Barbarian was here to monitor such an eventuality and adjusted the gas flow accordingly, slowing it down. But to his surprise the Barbarian suddenly said, "How 'bout this weather, huh?" It turned out all he wanted to do was have a pleasant chat about the rain, the forecast.

8.

The tinny office radio, by virtue of some unspoken edict, was set permanently to an odd station at the far end of the AM dial. It generated a continuous stream of big-band music and weird old songs he remembered his parents mentioning in passing: "Hernando's Hideaway" and "Nature Boy," along with Rosemary Clooney, who'd been his mother's particular favorite when she was younger. Francis had never chanced upon this radio station, not even once. There were no traces of it at home in Leedsville, which was only a half-hour from Tillman's. Jeanette, now immersed in all things radio, was also unaware of it. This dinky station seemed to have a broadcast range of around five miles and from what Francis could further ascertain, seemed to have around two disc jockeys.

Joe, along with his friend Norm, somehow managed to gain control over the even tinnier radio in the outside shed, cranking out the oldies station that more often than not broadcast the atrocious Skeeter Boss. The Skeeter Boss was a repellant DJ who'd been a big deal back in the 1950s and had, sadly, never gone away. He broadcast daily from his very own club in Margate, called—with characteristic lack of imagination—Skeeter's. His entire repertoire consisted of screeching *Clap your hands! Clap your hands! Clap your hands!* over and over while he blasted out the Shirelles or Martha and the Vandellas to the yelling, appreciative throng.

When Mr. Tillman would make his appearance, the radio—in the office and in the shed—would be unobtrusively turned off. This was never discussed; but the unofficial policy was that Mr. Tillman's visits would be unsullied by "Hernando's Hideway" or the ravings of the Skeeter Boss.

Francis, driving back and forth to the gas station, was now in his blue Chevette a good hour every day.

By sheer happenstance, he had stumbled upon the legendary Reverend Kirby McAdoo and his rambling, formless radio broadcasts. It had soon become an egregious listening habit. Kirby McAdoo had been a force since the 1930s, ensconced in his Cape May church and leading his passionate minions in endless battles against the myriad of enemies that were unraveling the moral fiber of the United States of America—communism, the Civil Rights movement, the tyranny of the federal government, Satanic influences. When Francis was in high school, the reverend had commandeered a parking lot near his church and actually commenced to burn a huge pile of rock and roll albums. The sheer anachronistic novelty of record-burning actually caught the brief attention of newspapers up and down the state and made it onto Philly TV.

Kirby McAdoo's grating, old man's voice was transmitted via a radio station that was as equally low-wattage as that station Sonny and Dutch favored. Francis imagined these two puny radio stations side by side, operating out of adjoining trailers in some field or next door to an ice-cream shack. This particular station, of course, was exclusively devoted to religion, devoid of secular enhancements like "Hernando's Hideaway."

Reverend Kirby McAdoo's broadcasts followed no discernible schedule or format. He simply got on the air and thundered away for as long as he wished. Two or three times McAdoo had broadcast from a pay phone. You could hear traffic in the background, the stray truck, McAdoo's asides to the operator. And Francis, for reasons he couldn't quite discern, found himself listening to Kirby McAdoo fulminate against Martin Luther King, the United Nations, the left-wing media. And then there was the Deuteronomy story, which McAdoo trotted out constantly. Many, many years ago, while preparing his weekly sermon, he had quite arbitrarily chanced upon a line from Deuteronomy: *Smite thee with madness.* And yet, upon reflection, was this really so arbitrary? Why had his eyes alighted on this very passage just when the nation was engaged in its greatest, most epochal struggle against the forces of anarchy and sin? Was not the hand of God evident in this supposedly random verse? The United States of America was being smitten with madness: the madness of paganism, obscenity, false idols.

Unfortunately, as Francis discovered, Kirby McAdoo was more boring than he was entertaining. His concern for the deteriorating moral fiber of the United States of America ultimately took second place to intricate, internecine religious disputes with other churches and clergy. These grievances seemed decades in the making, the lengthy tirades—brimming with names of ministers, councils, memoranda—a total mystery to the uninitiated. And it was these matters that, all in all, seemed to occupy the reverend's attention much more than the sinful world at large.

9.

He hadn't liked Dewey at first, who seemed offputtingly large, loud, and authoritative: The slicked-back hair, the glasses that reflected the reds, yellows, and whites of the car and station lights. Soon after Francis had begun his employment at Tillman's, a sudden thunderstorm had knocked out all the power and plunged the station and the Garden House into a pool of black. Dewey sprang into action, corralling the crew and forcing everyone to huddle near the shed. Rough and army-like, he brooked not a moment's hesitation. In this darkness, Dewey bellowed, a car could easily plow into all of them. And without the lights, an employee—off by himself, shirt pocket stuffed with a thick wad of cash—could be easily picked off and robbed. He'd seen it before, Dewey announced a good three times. And then he elaborated. Did they all think those cocksucker drivers weren't aware that there was lots and lots of cash around? Some of those fuckers would stop at nothing to rob a gas-station employee. Think he hadn't seen that? He sure as fuck *had* seen that. And those fancy cars shouldn't fool anyone, either. The drivers of those cars weren't better than him; they weren't better than anybody. When they took a shit, Dewey asserted, they smelled as bad as he did.

But Francis's opinion of Dewey, like that of Sonny, gradually shifted. Dewey had an aged, infirm mother and whenever older customers drove in, he assumed an entirely different persona: solicitous, respectful. He was also very funny, with a sense of irony that Francis had only associated with college circles. "Let's move some product," Dewey would exhort from time to time, a pitch-perfect lampoon of business-speak, urging Francis and all of them to do their best and maximize profit.

Dewey had an ex-wife and a daughter floating around somewhere. He had worked at Tillman's Gulf since the late 1960s. What a bastard Tillman was back then, he recounted. A real company man. In those days the full uniform involved a shirt buttoned all the way to the top and a regulation hat. The prick had made everyone adhere to these strictures even on the hottest days. As Mr. Tillman got older, though, he had eased up some, stopped shitting his pants at minor infractions.

However busy things got at the station was nothing, according to both Dewey and Sonny, compared to the gas crisis of a few years back. There had been, for a time, a three-dollar limit. How the fuck could you go *anywhere* on three dollars? Customers begged, cajoled, threatened. Some of the more enterprising and patient drivers simply drove to the end of the hideously long lines, waited out the sometimes half-hour crawl to the front, and got another three-dollar shot of gas, the attendants—loathe to play traffic cop—turning a blind eye to this little subterfuge.

At times the cars had been lined up almost to the Expressway, if you could believe that. Some of the other stations had actually run out of gas. Not Tillman's, though. An underground economy among some of the employees sprang up. Tips—a euphemism for "bribes"—in the amount of only a dollar or two, could guarantee circumventing the three-dollar limit with a six- or seven-dollar sale. Sometimes even ten dollars of gas could be procured, although getting away with dispensing that larger amount was tricky.

At the height of the crisis there were odd and even days—gas dispensed on the basis of whether one's last license-plate digit was odd or even. There was really no flouting this particular rule. Dewey, especially, enjoyed the customers who would announce to him that they were odd, of which he would emphatically agree. In the middle of the pandemonium this one customer, an elderly man, actually dropped dead, right there at Tillman's Gulf.

The irony, though, was that the unending flood of cars, which could turn the station into one large, horrible parking lot, conferred quite a bit of power on the crew. To begin with, the gas crisis was the focus of people's daily lives and a constant on the news; the subject of endless conversations. Tillman's Gulf was at the epicenter. The crew was not at the mercy of the odd-and-even tyranny, nor did they have to endure those endlessly long lines. In fact, they were the ones who controlled those endlessly long lines. To work at Tillman's was to wield power.

Depending on how lenient or enterprising an employee was feeling at any particular time, a customer could receive more than their allotted, paltry three dollars. And there was also an element of magnanimity, which mostly came from Dewey and Sonny: The limit quietly upped for the very old or those who seemed truly, really in need.

There was no washing windows, no checking the oil, no *May I help you?* In fact, it was the opposite of *May I help you?* The attendants were there to lay down the law: three-dollar limit, even or odd license plate. They catered to no one.

The odd and even days, of course, did not last. The limit increased to five dollars and then was phased out altogether. The chaos, the desperate drivers, the tips—these all quickly faded away. The normal equilibrium of a gas station began to return. *May I help you?* and *Fill 'er up* reentered the lexicon. The customers began to expect the washing of windows, the checking of oil, the giving of directions.

10.

The female beachgoers going to and fro yielded
endless opportunities to glimpse bathing suits, tanned
bodies, cleavage. Francis began to exhibit an extra diligence
in washing windows for these select customers.
Unfortunately, Vince had caught on to what Francis was
doing. He confided to Francis that he did exactly the same
thing. There was some discomfort in this: An inadvertent,
smutty solidarity with a crotch-scratching ex-sailor. The rest
of the crew, as a whole, were much more sedate about the
female customers than Francis had imagined. Long ago,
Dewey related, there was this one particular broad who had
strongly hinted at her agreeability to getting fucked by him
in the back parking lot. But those sort of accounts were
rare. Most everyone were married, meat-and-potatoes family
men.

Joe did mention, in passing, that the girls who came
into the station looked at you like you were nothing, and
Francis—speaking without thinking, as was often the
case—said it was probably because they assumed he was a
full-time gas-station employee. But, of course, Joe *was* a full-
time gas-station employee. And, no doubt, being a full-time
gas-station employee—or its equivalent—would forever be
his lot in life. In just this one sentence, Francis had
inadvertently handed Joe an insult, and in this same one
sentence, he had also separated himself from his inferiors:
Although Francis himself, technically, was also a full-time
employee at Tillman's Gulf, he was not a *full-timer*. He had
unintentionally let Joe know that he, Francis, occupied a
more enviable status. And then Francis tried, halfheartedly,
to explain his way out it, Joe listening indifferently.

Two older girls pulled into his lane, looking as if
they'd just come from the beach, slick with remnants of
suntan lotion, tanned and big-breasted, and Francis
instinctively grabbed the squeegee from the big bucket of

soapy water, but before he could begin his window-washing, he hit a small gas slick and tumbled completely off the island and onto the concrete. Most of the impact had been painfully absorbed in his right knee, and it was only the torrent of embarrassment that kept the pain from reaching an excruciating level. He hobbled off to the shed to nurse his physical pain and restore some of his tattered personal dignity, letting Norm handle the rest of the transaction.

The days were hot and packed with customers. The sun beat down on the silvery tops of the gas pumps. Eventually they would start to glisten, generating a surreal, halo-like glow.

There was a typically hot, hectic afternoon when Francis had finished up with what felt like his millionth customer. The gas had been dispensed, the money exchange made, the transaction unequivocally completed, yet the entire process must have been exceedingly mysterious to this driver, who hung his head out the window, awaiting words of instruction. "You can go now," Francis called out, politely but firmly, but the driver in Cliff's adjoining lane, a middle-aged woman, heard the words *You can go now*. And as if she were some sort of robot, programmed to obey simple directives without question, she sprang into action at this basic command, quickly starting her car and lurching forward.

Francis watched with a mixture of horror and fascination as the coiled hose—still dispensing gas—traveled through the air in what seemed like slow-motion, the hose tossed high into the air, a torrent of gasoline spewing forth, smashing against the woman's car and narrowly missing her windshield by mere inches, and then coming to rest on the concrete next to the pump. Nobody—not the hapless customer, not Cliff, not Francis—was injured. This was more egregious even than the last near-catastrophe, in which a brain-dead customer fecklessly tossed a lit, burning cigarette onto the gasoline-soaked concrete as Francis—with visions of Tillman's Gulf exploding in a fiery apocalypse worthy of a Kirby McAdoo sermon—took a running leap and stomped it out.

And then Vince did something equally idiotic. While grasping the gas hose and nattering on about god-knows-what, he inadvertently gave one long squeeze, sending a cascade of unleaded into the open window of the car directly behind him, soaking the backseat and its two occupants. The passengers, probably too stunned to fully process what had happened, were more magnanimous than one could have expected. The gasoline could have doused their faces; someone could have been smoking. Sonny, apprehensive about any possible legal ramifications, cleaned out the entire car—interior and exterior—and supplied a whole tank of gas, gratis.

The coup de grace, in terms of Vince's tenure at the station, came when he simply didn't show up for work one day and was promptly discharged.

He saw an Oregon license plate, a South Dakota, and—defying the laws of probability—two Utahs in one day, a few hours apart. A carload of people from Honduras. A contingent of Deadheads with *Jerry Saves* and *Best Band in the Land* regalia plastered all over the car. A dentist. An unbelievably effeminate man in a pink cutoff T-shirt, squealing his dismay at the weather forecast, which called for incipient rain. A large truck transporting chocolate-chip cookies, belching fumes. The truck was plastered with garishly colored, preternaturally jolly cookies. The driver himself, in dramatic contrast, was a nasty, rough-hewn type, barking out orders and impatiently demanding a receipt.

An older, polyester-clad man drove in, cursing excessively. Francis had begun to notice this intermittent phenomenon: Older men who seemed to assume that a salty vocabulary engendered some sort of bonding or solidarity with the gas-station attendant. It sure was a hot fucking day, this driver announced in a grating voice. His fucking car was almost out of fucking gas and probably the fucking oil needed to be checked as well. Sonny, overhearing this, was unimpressed. "That's some vocabulary, huh, kid?" he commented after the man had driven off.

One of Francis's many customers was Billy, of Billy's Used Auto Parts fame. The commercial for Billy's Used Auto Parts was ubiquitous; there probably wasn't a single day that TV-watchers could escape the herky-jerky animation of smiling tow trucks and engines, and then a modest, almost abashed-looking cartoon rendering of Billy himself, mouthing along to the chorus: *For a happy car/You don't have to go far/It's Billy's Used Auto Parts!* And now, here at Tillman's Gulf, was Billy in the flesh, looking similar indeed to his cartoon rendering; long hair and thick beard. Billy was surprisingly taciturn about his renown, explaining to Francis that he had nothing to do, really, with the commercial's concept and execution.

But an even bigger encounter awaited. None other than Larry Veniero himself drove into Francis's lane. Larry Veniero was a long-running fixture on Philly television, a spiffy, delicate-looking man with perfectly coiffed hair and impeccable suit and tie who played the organ every Sunday morning. The entire show consisted of Larry Veniero trotting out one chestnut after another, like "Roll Out the Barrel" or a John Philip Sousa ditty, the camera occasionally zooming around at different angles. Here was the top of Larry Veniero's head. Here was Larry Veniero at a side angle. A series of announcements scrolled continuously at the bottom of the screen: *Congratulations to Mr. and Mrs. Lou Accordino on their fiftieth wedding anniversary. Happy 90th birthday to Mrs. Edith Gomulka.*

Larry Veniero looked absolutely identical to his TV visage, asking for a full tank of gas and a receipt. A strange impulse took hold of Francis, who blurted out how much he liked his show. This was, of course, a complete absurdity. There was absolutely no way that anybody under the age of, say, sixty-five, could have watched Larry Veniero's show for longer than five minutes, much less have been an actual fan. But Larry Veniero accepted the compliment graciously. Francis was suddenly seized with an intense curiosity. Here was an unexpected opportunity to glean a bit of insight into the inner workings of Larry Veniero's life. Francis politely inquired—hoping it wasn't too impertinent—as to what his itinerary had been that day. And the answer was flabbergasting. He had, Larry Veniero informed Francis, spent the day visiting Admiral Neptune.

Admiral Neptune! Everyone had grown up watching Admiral Neptune. His show had started every day at 3:30, right after school had ended, and featured episodes of *Speed Racer*, jokes, and an Admiral Neptune birthday club. It boggled the mind that Larry Veniero and Admiral Neptune actually socialized together. What could they possibly talk about? Shoptalk, Francis imagined; the goings-on of the station. Or maybe more: Their hopes, their aspirations.

But Larry Veniero now had a full tank of gas and their interchange was coming to an end. Francis took his payment, made the appropriate change, and was thanked warmly. There was a brief pause. For a moment it seemed that Larry Veniero was going to deliver some profound parting words, but, in fact, Francis had simply forgotten to make out the requested receipt.

Dewey found the whole encounter vastly amusing, mentioning on several occasions the possibility of Francis and Larry Veniero getting to know each other better, of going on their first date.

12.

His parents, of course, were at the store during the day and Jeanette was off at the Rockin' Wave. Because of his crazy-quilt schedule, Francis often had the house to himself. His big indulgence was to order a sub to be delivered, which felt like an indolent pleasure. To his sorrow, Casa Enzo's, the high temple of cheesesteak subs, had shut its doors, and he was forced to cast about for a worthy successor. With a good deal of skepticism, he decided to venture forth into the newly opened Sal's. Sal's was housed, idiosyncratically, in what had been a tiny old church perched unobtrusively on Atlantic Heights Avenue. Their cheesesteaks, Francis had to admit, were a marvel to behold: almost the equal of Casa Enzo's, with the same sort of crusty bread and a skillful blending of raw onions, meat, cheese. A close runner-up to the legendary Casa Enzo's was no small thing, and so, accordingly, a few times a week an unsmiling, fat bearded man trudged out of his yellow car, carrying—depending on Francis's whim—a cheesesteak or pizzasteak, wrapped in an unending amount of thick white paper and then further encased in tinfoil, like binding a mummy. And Francis would eagerly consume his sub while aimlessly flicking through the TV channels.

That had been his perch back at Somerset Apartments, where he'd lived when he and Philip and Caleb had moved from the dorms and into town. Of course, the idea of food delivery would have been lunacy, what with the Brew 'n Wich and the deli just down the block, or the pizza place on the other side of Witherspoon Avenue. Ensconced in the apartment's massive, junky chair, his television watching had slowly grown exponentially. In due time, he had begun to watch until the middle of the night. Philip and Caleb would arise early, industriously cook their own breakfasts, and head into their morning classes. They would return to the apartment—having done all these things—just as Francis was getting up.

One afternoon, rooted as usual to the massive chair, Francis had watched the day's *Guiding Light*. *Guiding Light* was amazingly complex, with overlapping characters, deep traumas, and long-standing motifs. And then there was Vanessa, the sultry, scheming femme fatale who Francis had fallen in love with, eagerly awaiting her appearances. At the conclusion of today's episode, he had decided—in lieu of doing any schoolwork—to take in the afternoon movie: *The Interns* (1962), starring Cliff Robertson and Stefanie Powers. During a bloc of commercials he was gripped by a sudden, distinct feeling that he was dying. It was a tangible fear, although he truly wasn't in any sort of real peril. Yet the fear was there: A palpable wave of terror that coursed through his body, which he tried to tamp down by sitting stock-still. He managed to confine the fear to the left side of his head. That left side remained terrified, while the right side of his head remained relatively placid. He watched the rest of *The Interns* with a divided skull.

13.

Then there was Punch and Judy, the flipped-out couple who lived down the block from Somerset Apartments. They and a contingent of other like-minded oddballs had been riding around the country in a van, all of them from Oklahoma or Idaho or somewhere. Irreconcilable differences had landed Punch and Judy here while the rest had all gone on their way. Their very names—along with everything else about them—seemed like a trippy manifestation of mushroom ingestion or peyote buttons: Punch, actually, was the female; Judy was the male. Dubbing themselves Punch and Judy was designed to—in their own words—fuck with people's expectations.

Physically, Punch and Judy made for quite the pair. Punch was a wild-looking, unkempt girl with long, dirty-blond hair and an unwavering wardrobe of old jeans and formless peasant blouse that indicated large breasts. She was just this side of squat, while Judy was a tall, stick-thin apparition with uncombed, thinning long hair and reddish beard. His sartorial habits also were a constant: old, faded jeans and an even older blue T-shirt.

It was inevitable that Francis would get to know these two. He traversed Witherspoon fairly often and couldn't help but notice the distinctive duo, who—like him—appeared to have lots of free time.

They began chatting when they'd see each other. At times Francis took to visiting them in the evenings. Punch and Judy lived in a shabby apartment and Francis found their domicile intriguing. He had forgotten that people could exist outside of a college context. Even in their dirt-cheap circumstances, they had created the approximation of a home, proffering inedible, unsweetened cookies that Judy had baked or other wretched fare, like tofu, sprouts, black beans, washed down with anemic-tasting herbal tea. The food was served in chipped, cracked plates and bowls;

the tea in heavy, earth-colored mugs. Francis did his best to banish thoughts that Punch and Judy had obtained all this—including the silverware—via the Salvation Army or someone's trash.

It was all pleasant enough, though: The three of them hanging around in the apartment, listening to music, zoning out; occasionally getting high.

Judy was gainfully employed as a nude model for the college art department. His emaciated physique was, for some reason, in great demand for studies of the human form—that and the ability to remain stock-still for hours and hours at a time. The one occupational hazard, Judy related, was fighting the expected urge to get an erection. That could get difficult at times, requiring a good deal of mental gymnastics.

One evening at their little apartment Punch announced, without any preamble whatsoever, that she found Francis attractive and wished to have sex with him. It was uttered so plainly, so matter-of-fact, that for a moment he'd assumed he hadn't heard correctly. But of course he'd heard correctly. There was certainly no possibility of misconstruing *that*.

In theory, this should have been the pinnacle of his wildest erotic fantasies. A woman was blatantly offering herself to him. Now, though, that this was actually transpiring, he suddenly wished it was anybody but Punch who was doing the propositioning.

Then he remembered Judy, sitting impassively right here, in the middle of all of this. Francis was forced to ask him if it was okay to go off and have sex with his girlfriend, as if he was borrowing someone's car. It was indeed perfectly okay, Judy answered amicably, as long as he didn't have to hear any of the details—as if Francis would be inclined to enthusiastically report back to him. And in theory, two dudes discussing the parameters of fucking a girl—with the girl in attendance—seemed the height of sophisticated debauchery, but to Francis the overriding feeling was one of awkwardness.

Having secured Judy's blessings, there was really no other option but for him and Punch to depart, exiting the domicile and making their way to Somerset Apartments. True to form, Punch was wearing her old jeans and familiar peasant shirt. He was instantly aware of her slight heftiness, the unkempt manner. There was the nagging feeling of not wishing to be observed by anyone, wincing inwardly whenever a car passed by. And then, as the apartment loomed ever closer, Francis began an imploring, silent prayer that Philip and Caleb were far away; far, far away— maybe, even, out of the country. And these prayers were answered. The apartment, at least for now, was empty.

Punch annoyed him right off the bat by pulling out a few of his albums—without permission—and putting one on the turntable. Then she jumped up and down on the bed, which annoyed him further. He had no patience, really, for her whimsy. Then Punch removed all her clothing. She was hairier than he'd imagined; legs covered with a crop of black hair. Her breasts were indeed large, which only augmented her chunkiness. He had no choice but to disrobe as well, fumbling around for the pack of condoms he kept around for basically cosmetic reasons—making himself feel like the lothario who needed protection at a moment's notice. And in this instance, it *was* a moment's notice and he *did* need protection.

He was seized with indecision. Should he kiss her? He elected not to. Punch, it could be discerned now, used no deodorant. Without preamble, they had sex. He climaxed in around two minutes. Punch seemed unfazed, dressing quickly and—as if this had been a date at the movies—said that it had been fun and they should do it again.

Civility required that he walk her to the front entrance, partly out of chivalry and partly to ensure that she was, in fact, leaving. Punch exited, took a few steps toward

Witherspoon, and then in a loud, laughing voice that could be heard in every apartment in the Somerset Apartments complex, in a voice that certainly carried over into every dorm room, classroom, and boomed out over University Avenue, urged him not to shoot his load so quickly next time.

14.

In the wake of Vince's unceremonious departure, a gap developed, with Norm filling in as best he could until a permanent replacement could be found. Extra help—most of them entirely forgettable—floated in and out. The only real exception was that large, Lurch-like fill-in whose name Francis had never bothered to ascertain; a morose, taciturn type who either operated in brooding silence or trotted out an endless series of jokes, most of which revolved around the theme of penis enlargement.

The permanent replacement, soon enough, was Eddie. Eddie was loud, prone to declaiming on all sorts of matters large and small. The details of his life were fuzzy, the facts and chronology shifting during Eddie's retellings. He had been in the Marines—and not just a mere recruit, either, but a feared and respected drill instructor. And he had been stripped of this position, Eddie recounted with no uncertain pride, for a brutality even excessive by the tough standards of the Corps. There were strong intimations of cloak-and-dagger activity as well—covert missions—which he still wasn't at liberty to discuss.

Eddie was fresh from the hot-dog wars. His previous position had been manning one of the hot-dog carts in Atlantic City. These carts—hitherto an unknown commodity in Atlantic City—had suddenly proliferated during the past year. Two hot-dog cart outfits—apparently bitter rivals—had laid claim to this new turf. A vicious fight for dominance ensued, involving threats and lawsuits. Eventually the rancor escalated into outright violence. The hot-dog wars—as the *Journal-Bulletin* and everyone else dubbed it—took on the form of overturned carts, vandalized supply trucks. Hundreds of ketchup packets were torn open, their thick, red contents deposited on a side street.

The hot-dog wars grew even more sordid. The advent of legalized gambling and rise of the casinos had ushered in a wave of prostitutes, garishly-clad hookers perched up and down Pacific Avenue. Some of these scarlet women had been enlisted by both factions of the hot-dog belligerents, utilized for purposes of entrapment and god knew what else.

Not surprisingly, Eddie had been—according to his retellings—at the forefront of the hot-dog battles, manning his cart with a gutsy fearlessness, daring one and all to come fuck with him. And nobody, of course, was foolish enough to even try. Soon he was feared far and wide. And his bravado did not even stop with the police, poseurs that they were. In fact, Eddie was bold enough and unafraid enough to march right up to a cop's face, look him right in the eye, and loudly assert: "You ain't *shit* without your uniform."

Francis had assumed that Joe and Norm, both veterans of Vietnam, might display a bit of affinity for the new warrior-employee, but they both maintained a wary distance. Although Cliff and Eddie were brother Marines, Cliff too kept his distance. This made sense. Cliff was unfailingly closemouthed about his stint in the Marines, providing absolutely no details. He would certainly be disinclined to share his experiences with the likes of Eddie.

At some point, like a button had been pushed, Eddie became instantly pious, the anecdotes of beating the fuck out of some recruit or defending his hot-dog cart entirely replaced by exhortations to read the Bible, to go to church. It was impossible to piece toegether if Eddie, all along, had been harboring this religious fervor or if he had launched into an entirely new persona. "Oh, *go to church!*" Eddie would exhort in general from time to time, Francis never quite ascertaining what this meant or who it was meant *for*, exactly. And Cliff—who, after all, was studying to be an evangelist—seemed even more wary of Eddie than before. Yet Eddie, somehow, was a perfectly functioning, competent Tillman's employee, both attentive and courteous to the customers.

15

Francis's practice, driving to and fro from work, was to scan the radio dial, enjoying the potpourri of the disparate stations: Kirby McAdoo to classical to oldies to WMMR—everyone's mainstay FM station—and then back to the news, classical, WMMR. His listening included, of course, the Rockin' Wave. Jeanette's repertoire, he was happy to hear, had increased. Not only was her Kicks spot aired at semi-regular intervals, but she had hatched a new ad as well, this one for Toohey's Fish Fry in Ocean City. Toohey's had been around forever and they were now desirous of spiffing up their image. Accordingly, a brassy, updated jingle—Jeanette's brainchild—began making its appearance on FM 96.

FM 96 was in the grips of yet another intensive debate on potentially rejiggering its image. There was now a push by some to change *Rockin' Wave* to the more exuberant *Rockin' Wave!* with the hope that the crucial addition of an exclamation point would undergird the intrinsic excitement that came from listening to FM 96. And then again, there was Jeanette's inevitable, forced comparison that was designed to make Francis feel better: Her earnest query if *his* particular station ever felt the need to change its image, to attract a whole new range of consumers, to broaden its base. But Tillman's certainly had its base covered—state troopers, Barbarians, confused tourists, Larry Veniero. The addition of an exclamation point to Tillman's Gulf— *Tillman's Gulf!*—would be superfluous.

Jeanette had been the one to lead the charge against the insertion of the exclamation point. It was, she argued, too forced, too self-consciously colloquial. And then there would be the time and expense of altering the station's logos and promotional copy—all for something that would, most likely, yield incremental benefits to the station. Her viewpoint prevailed. The Rockin' Wave—simple and unadorned, without an exclamation point—remained intact.

On one of his meanderings through the radio dial, he settled upon the classical station. A few minutes later, Elgar's *Pomp and Circumstance* thundered out of the car radio. He was stunned to hear it in its entirety, so radically out of context: Not part of any college commencement, but here in his Chevette. It had never really occurred to him, until now, that *Pomp and Circumstance* was an actual piece of music.

From its first melodic flourishes, Francis was overcome with an intense, overpowering wave of emotion. *Pomp and Circumstance*, he was now able to ascertain, was both melodious and somber, suffused with an air of quiet intensity, a melancholy both wistful and bittersweet. By the time that stately, recognizable theme wafted out and floated throughout the car, he was near tears.

That stately, recognizable theme. It was not simply a musical piece that was traditionally played at commencement, but the aural leitmotif of their entire four years of study and life experience, denoting a swirl of emotions and memories. Think, *Pomp and Circumstance* was saying, of all that has happened to you during these past four years. Think of all that was being left behind. And then the genius of Elgar's piece was that, along with those feelings, was an equal overlay of hopes and dreams. Think of what was to come. Think of your world of possibilities.

The rest of Francis's drive home was spent in a sort of daze, a tangle of evocative feelings and memories. But those evocative feelings and memories were pegged to a rite of passage that was entirely imaginary: His college graduation, which had never happened.

The next day, as if possessed, he drove to the mall and paid a visit to Shoresounds, the record store that had once been such a central locus for him and his friends. Shame began to gnaw at him as he made his way to the small classical section off in the corner. As if he was attempting to buy contraband or a copy of *Hustler*, he hurriedly managed to ascertain that *Pomp and Circumstance* was, yes, in stock, which he purchased shamefacedly, exposing his deepest, most private self in full view of everyone at Shoresounds. He smuggled the album into the house, hiding it among his other albums.

Pomp and Circumstance filled the house when the rest of the family was gone. It often accompanied his cheesesteak or pizzasteak, and when it played Francis wandered into a world where he carefully donned his graduation gown, graduation cap precariously perched, tassels bouncing around.

All of them were assembled under the hot sun. Anticipation was building. Amused, knowing glances were exchanged as the commencement speakers droned on and on, trotting out those timeworn platitudes. They were timeworn, to be sure, but also—in their own way—comforting as well.

Did graduates really toss their caps into the air? If so, that would have been much too whimsical for him. Even in the midst of this joyous rite of passage, it would have been necessary for him to maintain a slight bit of reserve. Cap-tossing was not for him, although Annie would no doubt urge him to. And why not? Why not just this once?

His parents and Jeanette, as well, took one photo after another, preserving this day for posterity. And then there was the requisite dinner at, of course, the Leafcup, the venerable restaurant only a few blocks from Witherspoon Avenue, but metaphorically hundreds of miles away from Somerset Apartments. The grand old building was surrounded by a grassy expanse, the pastoral setting framed by the restaurant's gleaming wooden exterior with its white columns and beckoning portico. On an occasion as momentous as graduation dinner, he and his father would certainly be appareled in suit and tie. Annie would look flushed and happy. The Leafcup would be packed with fellow graduates and their parents. What a long, intensive time it had been; a complicated four years of hard work, tears, triumph.

A basket of hot rolls, wrapped in thick, white napkins, would be placed on their table, pats of butter on the side. Wisps of steam would emanate from the fragrant bread. Graduation dinner at the Leafcup would involve thick glasses of iced water, heavy silverware laid out, and then menus, appetizers, the dinner itself, drinks, coffee. Here, amid the hubbub of the Leafcup, he and Annie would smile at each other, exchange a few words.

16.

Working at Tillman's had engendered, to his surprise, the emergence of a thick, dark callus on his right hand that ran from thumb to forefinger, like the byproduct of some particularly vigorous masturbatory practice. The calloused skin, of course, was brought on by the constant grasping and squeezing of the gas hose, and this dark swath of skin would catch him unawares, arbitrarily coming to his attention at random moments—driving, eating a sub, watching TV. Along with this momentary surprise would be a flush of shame. His tenure at Tillman's Gulf was actually producing a physical manifestation. And mixed in with those feelings of shame was also a contradictory sort of pride as well: The callus was evidence of his workingman's life.

To his intense joy, that tough-looking cashier from the Garden House appeared in his lane, as if materializing out of thin air, and he instinctively glanced down at his calloused hand, as if to fortify himself to speak with her. Here he was, the rough-and-tumble sort who pumped gas all day long, used improper grammar, and then went out to some biker bar until three in the morning. But by the time he actually made contact with her a few moments later, the tough, rough-hewn worker had once again been subsumed by the timid college boy. She was surprisingly friendly, this tough Garden House cashier, but the entire encounter was nothing but anticlimactic. As cheery as this cashier was, she remained businesslike, not inclined to linger, thanking him warmly for his help and then zipping off in her little car.

The callus on his right hand produced mixed feelings, but what gave him absolutely unambiguous disgust was that working at Tillman's had tanned his arms to a far, far greater degree than the rest of his body. This was the dreaded shoobie tan. *Shoobie* was the derisive tag for the swarms of those annoying, ridiculous tourists who invaded the shore each and every summer, clogging the roads with their inept, clueless driving, shamelessly flaunting their laughingly inappropriate beach garb. The most egregious, most easily identifiable shoobie transgression was their futile attempts at an acceptable tan, which yielded that telltale white skin and those sun-darkened arms.

And now this was Francis's lot. He, who had spent so many summers carefully crafting a suntan, was now reduced to the shameful shoobie tan of darkened arms and light body. On his days off from Tillman's, he commenced with a tanning regimen that necessitated frequenting the beaches of Ocean City, Margate, Longport.

He had practically lived on the beach during all those summers past. They all did; half of Leedsville High School, it felt like, swarming out onto the sand and laying claim to the best stretches, positioning themselves for optimum sun exposure, concocting the elaborate schemes to avoid the obtrusive beach-tag inspectors.

Those days were all a thing of the past. Yet, to his relief, the comforting touchstones still existed. Lucy the Elephant, the giant elephantine figure that had once, way back when, been a hotel, still stood guard over the Margate beach. In Ocean City, those noisy biplanes still clattered over the ocean, their advertising banners streaming out the back in full view, alerting the beachgoers as to fish-fry specials, popular bars, various discounts, clambakes. The boardwalk was, as usual, jammed with vacationers, the cornucopia of food and drink eternally in evidence: pizza, lemonade, soft ice cream, saltwater taffy, fudge, funnel cakes. The seagulls still cawed.

Francis had some friends scattered about; a few, not many. He was not all that inclined to seek them out. Throughout college he'd been in fairly close contact with many of his social circle, keeping in touch throughout the school year and reconnecting during summer vacations. And now he was back home, working at Tillman's Gulf.

Art had been one of his best friends at Leedsville High. He had undergone a sudden personality shift as soon as he entered college, with a latent tendency toward pomposity coming to the fore. Art was full of grandiose, ever-shifting plans: law school, graduate school, the foreign service. None of these had come to even remote fruition. Now Art had immersed himself as a manager-trainee at the Dover Hotel, its dazzlingly bright-pink stucco exterior visible even before you crossed the bridge into Ocean City.

It appeared that Art had an unexpected flair for hotel management. To Francis's amazement, he took to wearing a tie even in his off hours. He began attending trade shows. Much of his conversations now—akin to Jeanette at the Rockin' Wave—revolved around the inner workings of the Dover, which were surprisingly byzantine. The hotel was owned by two brothers who were engaged in a lifelong sibling rivalry, each with his own quirks and idiosyncrasies, each brother heading his own informal faction.

Art's stories about the Dover had a vague, nebulous undercurrent that made it difficult to decipher what, exactly, his job duties really were. Francis had begun to suspect—to hope, actually—that Art was, in reality, no more than a glorified flunky.

Francis, of course, was not part of any management-trainee program. He did take some small, amused consolation in the fact that there was a certain amount of limited celebrity status attached to being a Tillman's Gulf employee. He'd been on the Ocean City boardwalk, ready to descend upon the beach, when he was suddenly accosted by a loud, bubbly female who seemed positively overjoyed to have spotted him. This was, to be sure, an exhilarating ego boost, but it was also disorienting and slightly disconcerting. He struggled to ascertain this odd girl's identity. As it turned out, he had waited on her at the station two nights past, one customer in a sea of unending cars. Apparently, she had been en route to an Ocean City vacation, gas tank almost empty, when she'd pulled into Tillman's and gotten fuel from him, this helpful, friendly attendant. He did remember her—very vaguely, to be sure—but with the noblesse oblige of the true celebrity, he professed to remember her vividly, as if working at Tillman's Gulf really hadn't been a hot, continuous blur of car after car after car.

And then it happened again some time after that, right by Lucy the Elephant: Two grizzled older men, both sporting outlandish, fluorescent beachwear, who hailed him warmly and offered him a cigarette. For a brief moment, it had seemed as if some sort of con was about to be perpetrated on him, but then he suddenly remembered—also vaguely—waiting on these two men a few days before.

Cliff, too, he related to Francis, had been recognized in public from time to time. Francis had found Cliff to be good-natured and exceptionally funny, belying whatever stereotypes he'd harbored when it came to the super-religious. Francis's own exposure was basically confined to hearing Kirby McAdoo's exploits and to the likes of Brother Jess Tutt. Brother Jess Tutt and his anemic-looking wife, Sister Cecily, popped up—uninvited and unannounced—at college campuses across the nation. On this one day, they planted themselves in the midst of the commons and Brother Jess commenced with a thunderous, X-rated tirade against the lust, fornication, and general debauchery pulsating throughout the university. A few students had tried to shout down Brother Jess Tutt, but Brother Jess, not to be stymied, redoubled his volume. Things got even noisier. Brother Jess, to Francis's surprise, actually had some sympathizers among the commons throng. His defenders launched their own verbal counterattack. Sister Cecily began singing. A near-riot ensued. The campus police were summoned and Brother Jess and Sister Cecily—each holding their Bibles aloft—were sent packing.

A church bus pulled into Tillman's, and while Francis was pumping gas Cliff conferred privately with some of the passengers, deliberately misinforming them that Francis was eager for prayers to be directed his way, but was entirely too bashful to make the request himself. And so, as the bus pulled away, Francis was the recipient of a fervent chorus of *God bless yous* erupting from the open windows.

Joe, as affable as he was, had nevertheless incorporated a little dose of military spit-and-polish into the running of Tillman's Gulf, utilizing army terminology in the recording of license plates during credit-card transactions. He had taken, soldier-style, to calling out the plate letters as *delta-november-hotel*; *oscar-alpha-papa*. Francis began to institute his own special nonsense terminology: *noodle-vomit-cabbage*—which Cliff picked up on immediately—to the confusion on the part of some customers, unaccustomed as they were to hearing what sounded like total gibberish bandied about by gas-station employees.

As irreverent and funny as Cliff was, Francis was slightly taken aback when Cliff had casually offered him an invite to a fellowship dinner. He had instinctively trotted out some fumbling excuse and Cliff didn't pursue it.

17.

One of the codes of conduct at Tillman's Gulf was to turn in inebriated drivers to the lawful authorities. Those sort of drivers were, to be sure, a rarity, but it did happen a few times on Francis's watch. The first instance involved a middle-aged man who seemed visibly, overtly shitfaced, slurring his words, head dropping into his lap, reeking of alcohol. Joe instructed Francis to keep the drunk occupied while he ran into the office and made a call to the troopers.

This seemed repulsive. The state troopers, to Francis, seemed like authoritarian zealots, especially this one younger, mustached enforcer who had expressed incredulity at witnessing Francis service an older black customer's fancy car. The trooper shook his head in sincere bewilderment. "Man," he queried aloud after the car had pulled away, "where'd that nigger get the money to buy a car like that?"

And there was the larger issue. When had he ever sided with cops? But then one afternoon he was jolted by the sounds of hooting and hollering coming from a customer. It was a guy his own age who had stopped his car, taking up the space of two pumps, and then got out, circling the pumps and babbling away, unable even to ask for gasoline. With a vindictive zeal he hadn't known he'd even possessed, Francis took down the license-plate number, ran into the office, and called the troopers.

There was a brief moment of confusion as he instinctively read off the plate letters using his own special code that lampooned Joe's army terminology—*pruneface-garbage*, in this case—but he quickly corrected himself to the nonplussed dispatcher, ratting out this hooting, hollering driver too zonked to even put a sentence together. That driver, Francis was informed around an hour later by one of the troopers, had been duly apprehended—and with illegal substances found in the car. There was a moment of strong unease: this driver, whoever he was, was certainly facing

grave consequences—grave consequences ensuing from
Francis's one, simple phone call to the state troopers. Then
the unease faded. That driver could have plowed into
another car, caused a serious accident, fatalities. Perhaps
Francis, with this one phone call, had saved the life of an
innocent family. Now he felt akin to an avenging angel, the
righter of wrongs. He would help keep the Expressway safe.

The sternest, strongest exponent of turning in those
drivers under the influence—indeed, the sternest, strongest
exponent of following a perceived Tillman's Gulf code of
conduct—was a humorless mandarin whom Francis had
dubbed Lord Haw-Haw. The appellation was in honor of
his braying, piercing laugh, a continuous series of *haw-haw-
haws*, followed by the shake of the head and, in conclusion,
an *I'll tell ya*, as if he couldn't get over his own innate wit.
And there was the added, private satisfaction that Lord
Haw-Haw was the name of the infamous British
collaborator during the Second World War.

The Lord Haw-Haw of Tillman's Gulf was
schoolmarmish and hectoring. He claimed, in his quavery
voice, that he felt no qualms whatsoever about approaching
girls and asking them, point-blank, if they would go out with
him. Their answer, as far as Francis could best determine,
seemed to be *no*.

Lord Haw-Haw had also asserted, more than once,
that he laid down the law when it came time for customers
to turn off their engines, presenting a blunt ultimatum: Turn
off your engine or you get no gas. Francis had never
personally witnessed this display of Lord Haw-Haw's iron
will. He also had strongly opined to Francis on the only
correct, truly effective method of washing windows: Start at
the very top; work steadily downward in a series of neat,
well-defined strokes, which—if one took the proper care—
reduced the risk of smudges, if not eliminating them
altogether. Lord Haw-Haw offered further unsolicited,

unwanted advice on how best to organize one's roll of money and the most effective technique as to how to avoid spilling a single drop of gas. He was the only Tillman's employee who Francis really detested.

It was his misfortune to work alongside Lord Haw-Haw on a hot morning when the station was packed with car after car. For the hundredth fucking time that day, it felt like, Francis was required to grab the squeegee, shake off the excess water, and prepare to wash yet another windshield. Suddenly, to his mild annoyance, the air was filled with the warbling sound of Lord Haw-Haw's voice: "Start from the bottom!"

This was Lord Haw-Haw's idea of a joke: Entertaining the notion of actually washing a window contra the established procedure. Francis paused momentarily, sifted through the array of potential responses, and then—drawing a blank—went back to the task at hand. But his brief hesitancy had been thoroughly misinterpreted. "You was going to do it!" Lord Haw-Haw shouted at Francis in delighted triumph. "You was going to do it! You was going to start from the bottom!"

And then came the expected *haw-haw-haw*, followed by another *haw-haw-haw* blast. Francis was startled into laughter, which Lord Haw-Haw incorrectly took to mean that Francis was laughing *with* him, not at him. And that assumption was entirely erroneous, of course. Francis's laughter spurred Lord Haw-Haw on all the more: *haw-haw-haw-haw-haw*, a continuous barrage, and Francis, startled anew, began laughing some more, which became the catalyst for more *haw-haw-haws*.

This time Lord Haw-Haw's laugher continued unabated, unchecked by the pro forma *I'll tell ya*. Francis, wishing he were somewhere else entirely, glanced around. A look of utter astonishment could be glimpsed on some of the customers' faces. One woman in particular had a look of outright alarm, staring at Lord Haw-Haw with a look that

Francis had only seen when the station was overrun with Barbarians.

Later, when there was a brief respite, Francis hurried over to the Philly-bound lane, where Cliff was working. He found Cliff off to the side of a pickup truck, dispensing gas. As Francis approached, he called out to Cliff that something had happened earlier; something so funny he wouldn't believe it. The driver of the pickup—window wide open—had forgotten about Cliff's existence and assumed that Francis was addressing *him*. "What happened?" the driver asked Francis with real curiosity, finding it entirely plausible that a random gas-station attendant would arbitrarily approach him to relate some amusing bit of news about the day.

18

Toby Hunt's, the fabled bar and music venue perched on the bay, was gone. Francis and so many of them had spent a great deal of time at Toby Hunt's, some of it while blatantly underage. The disconcerting news of its demise had reached Francis right before he left college. Toby Hunt's had been the loud, rowdy centerpiece of the even louder, even rowdier beer-soaked clubs that ran up and down Bay Street.

It had been the largest and most popular of them all, an imposing structure that framed the entrance to Bay Street, facing out over the bay and then, in the opposite direction, out to the Mainland Diner and the frenetic traffic circle that fed into the bridge to Ocean City. And from Bay Street one could gaze out at Ocean City, the Wondertime Pier's multi-colored, mammoth Ferris wheel that framed the sky; the Dover Hotel.

The rest of the clubs, though, were still extant—the Parlor, Bayhouse, the Rockery; all of them plying their ear-splitting music and cheap alcohol. On one memorable occasion, Francis had puked his guts out in the parking lot after the Parlor's seven-beers-for-a-buck weekly special.

The distinctive, boxy shape of Toby Hunt's was still in evidence, but the new management had done their level best to obliterate any associations with the building's previous, sweaty incarnation. Now there was a glass-fronted, pinkish monstrosity with its new name—Plush—in huge, glowing red neon.

Both he and Art had been curious to check out this new venue. And so they did, but as they approached the entrance, an unexpected sense of discomfort began to percolate. Suddenly it seemed as if entering this place called Plush was more fraught with uncertainty than those days of sneaking into Toby Hunt's when they were under the legal drinking age. That, at least, was part of a venerable, enshrined tradition of trying to successfully connive one's way into the Point's bars. And the trepidation, all in all, was minimal. There were really only two possibilities: Either you got in or you didn't.

Even the neon *Plush* seemed discombobulating. Bay Street had no need for fancy neon signs. Did Toby Hunt's even *have* a sign at all? Francis strained to remember. Toby Hunt's had been so renowned, so recognizable, that it had no need whatsoever to scream out its name in ostentatious signage. Toby Hunt's exhibited a quiet confidence.

Entering Plush was immediately confusing. That huge stage where one thunderous, high-volume band after another had performed was gone. Zag, Francis suddenly remembered, the loutish lead singer of Mountain Grown, had leaned precariously into the audience, passing around his open bottle of Southern Comfort so fans could take a swig. It had been one of the most revolting things he had ever seen. Thinking about it, even now, made him sick to his stomach.

He and Art gradually recovered their bearings. Not each and every trace of Toby Hunt's had been obliterated. The huge bar that ran across the middle, almost bisecting Toby Hunt's, had been greatly reduced in size, but it still existed, providing a navigational touchstone. From there it was possible for Francis and Art to loosely orient themselves.

There were tables and chairs spread throughout the back. Plush, they came to realize, served appetizers. Tables, chairs, and appetizers—indeed, any sort of food whatsoever—were unknown quantities at Toby Hunt's. One didn't sit at Toby Hunt's. One stood. And if you wanted to offset your massive alcohol intake with some food, this was not the place. You could, if need be, stagger over to the diner, crossing the busy traffic circle, taking care to avoid getting hit by a car or bus.

Plush billed itself as a dance club. It certainly lived up to its name, the darkened main area full of gyrating bodies responding to hideous mechanical music. A mass of coiffed people, men and women both, were streaming to and from the dance floor. Art should have worn a tie; he would have fit right in, but the loud volume made it impossible to communicate these—or any other—thoughts.

The crowd obviously loved this wretched music, dancing with gleeful, full-throttled abandon. As their eyes adjusted to the darkness, he and Art grew acclimatized to the Plush scene, with some of the nuances becoming apparent. They were not, it turned out, the only non-participants in the dancing. Many others hovered nearby, sticking to the sidelines, unwilling or unable to join in the general revelry. These amorphous, shadowy shapes gradually assumed a more definite form, including an older woman who, to Francis's surprise, caught his eye and delivered a wide, inviting smile.

They smiled at each other through the dance floor's flashing lights. A jolt of sexual electricity shot through his very being. An older woman at a dance club had intrinsically erotic connotations, although he had no idea what, exactly, those erotic connotations were. Uncertainty gripped him. The protocol here at Plush was a mystery. He was in a foreign land. Before he could process all this, the woman edged over to him and asked if he wanted to dance.

Absolutely avoiding meeting Art's gaze, he dutifully trotted out to the dance floor, awash with a sudden insecurity. Nobody ever danced at Toby Hunt's or at the Parlor, Bayhouse, Rockery. He couldn't recall a single time he'd ever actually ventured onto a dance floor, even at the Harmony. If he had, it was under circumstances of extreme inebriation. When the music flowed forth now, though, he saw that his trepidation was unfounded. The Plush dance floor was so jammed full that only perfunctory movement was even possible. Slow dancing, he quickly comprehended, was an accepted practice here, and so he and this older woman linked together, moving along with the horde of others. She was taller than he was, her small breasts occasionally making contact with his body, the encounter rendered almost entirely anonymous by the lack of lighting and her long hair cascading over her face, the top-volume music that made it impossible to converse.

It was unbelievably crowded on this dance floor. The smell of this woman's sweet, vaguely exotic perfume drifted into the music. Intrusive mirrors were placed throughout, but the last thing he wanted to glimpse was a reflection of his own dancing. Another slow song started and they pressed into each other. The erotic possibilities suddenly seemed infinite, almost unimaginable; although what, in fact, those erotic possibilities would be he couldn't begin to guess. Would they go immediately to her place of residence? They danced some more; fast and slow dances. The fast dancing was not so awful if one could avoid the mirrors, if you could try not to think too hard about your actions. He fervently hoped that Art had disappeared. There was some more dancing. Then, to his surprise, the last dance was announced. Had he spent the whole evening dancing with this perfumed older woman? They again locked together and jarring, bright light flooded the dance floor. Plush was closing.

It was startling now to see his dance partner without the cloak of darkness. She was a good deal older than he'd imagined, lines and wrinkles crisscrossing her face. Before he could fully process this, a man and woman of roughly her age materialized, the man in shiny dark pants and an even shinier dark-green shirt. The woman had on a good deal of makeup. She and Francis's dance partner conversed briefly in a foreign tongue, which he was unable to identify. There was no trace, as far as he could tell, of Art.

His new, odd social circle was certainly an affable bunch. It was decided to brave the traffic circle and walk over to the Mainland Diner. Drivers, even at this later hour, sped their way through the various chaotic lanes of the circle, a steady stream of car lights stretching and blinking their way from here to the bridge. The buses now were probably done for the night, which made the crossing slightly less of a mad dash to safety. The four of them crossed the traffic circle in a quick trot, making it safely to the other side.

The diner was agreeably crowded, booths and tables mostly full; the low hum of steady conversation, occasional burst of laughter. A pleasant sense of fatigue overtook him as they made their way to their booth, this strange foursome he'd somehow managed to become a part of. The cheery older waitress proffered the thick, shiny diner menus. They ordered coffee, food: cinnamon toast, muffins. He realized, at that moment, that he had neglected to ask for his dance partner's name. Or perhaps her introduction was lost in Plush's cacophony. It was too late now. He could hear orders shouted into the kitchen, the doors opening and closing, the bustle of waitresses running back and forth. The air abounded with a diner's typical jumble of scents: coffee and dinner and breakfast and dessert.

An entirely arbitrary memory flashed through Francis's mind: He had been sitting at the commons, eating his lunch, when it became horrifyingly apparent that he was choking to death—right now, right here in the commons. He half-rose from the table in a lurching panic and then just as suddenly realized he was not, in fact, choking at all. He sat back down, drenched in fear and misery. All this had gone entirely unnoticed. In reality, the whole episode had lasted a few seconds. The commons chugged along at its normal pace and volume; the chatter and laughter, the clink of utensils.

***

The waitress brought their orders. His choice of toasted corn muffin—an elaborate concoction that involved melted butter slathered over the middle, oozing out onto the plate—received a favorable reaction from his new friends. The man in the shiny green shirt—whose name was also a mystery—expressed mild regret at his own choice of blueberry muffin. He should have, he said, ordered a corn muffin instead.

Francis's Plush dance partner was indeed older, as were this man and woman, who seemed to be husband and wife. The two women again conversed briefly in a foreign tongue. They were from Portugal, he learned, and listened with interest to the cadences of the language, a sound altogether different—almost guttural—from the lilting Brazilian variant he knew from the music.

She cleaned rooms, Francis learned, at various motels in Ocean City. So he had spent the night dancing with a cleaning woman, which gave him pause. Her daughter was twenty and worked in Cape May.

The conversation then turned to the weather. So far, they had all been spared a heat wave, although the advent of a heat wave as the summer progressed certainly was a strong theoretical possibility. You never knew when a heat wave would strike, how long it would last. The affable man in the shiny green shirt was impressed with the diner's steady volume of business. Their locale was a gold mine, perched as it was by the traffic circle and Bay Street. Everyone knew the Mainland Diner.

Francis felt his lust recede and vanish altogether. A companionable silence settled over the booth. They ordered more coffee. The woman from Portugal who cleaned motel rooms in Ocean City switched to tea; the hot, lemony odor a sharp contrast to the coffee and muffins.

19

Within the space of an hour, two mammoth trucks came into Francis's lane. Trucks of this immensity were a steady—albeit infrequent—commodity at Tillman's. Two in one day, and at such close intervals, were almost unheard of. These trucks necessitated a great deal of effort, an entire lane blocked off as the huge vehicle maneuvered into position, Francis half fearful and half hopeful that the driver would somehow miscalculate and plow into the pumps. It never came close to happening, of course. These expert drivers were able not just to maneuver into position, but also to align perfectly with the diesel hose.

So giant were some of these trucks that they could actually blot out the shining sun. It took forever to fill up the massive, seemingly bottomless gas tank, the steady *click-click-click* of the pump's price gauge going on and on and on, tallying up an astronomical total; gallons upon gallons, the process taking such a long time that on occasion the driver would saunter over to the Garden House and come back with food and drink, or take the opportunity to stand off to the side and smoke a cigarette, chatting with Sonny or Dewey or Dutch, the *click-click-click* a steady backdrop. The strong, not unpleasant odor of diesel permeated the space around the gas pump, the sort of odor that one could come into contact with while traveling on the highway, but now this same smell existed in a different, stationary context, as if a chunk of highway driving had momentarily reappeared here.

That day of the two trucks was also the day that Lon came into the station. Francis and Lon had been improbable best friends back in eighth grade. Lon was famous school-wide for his wild ways, but that year Francis discovered that Lon was not just exceptionally funny, but also possessed an enormous reservoir of insight and perception. And so, that year in eighth grade, he and Lon had become inseparable.

Even Francis's father, usually so indifferent to his and Jeanette's friends trooping in and out, had developed an affinity for—of all people—Lon.

When ninth grade started, the friendship had been dashed upon the shoals of high school. Leedsville High funneled students into their delineated, codified slots, with Francis, of course, on the pre-college path and Lon on the polar opposite. They were in none of the same classes. Both he and Lon returned to their gravitational pulls, the improbable friendship quickly evaporating. As high school progressed he remained dimly aware of Lon's existence. Lon, he knew, had graduated with the rest of them. Then Francis lost track of him completely.

The oddest thing was that Lon's instinctive, untutored insight carried over for far, far longer than Francis ever imagined. In eighth grade, Lon had delivered a précis on the difference between cute, pretty, and beautiful—citing specific girls from the class as examples. It was something Francis found himself unwittingly referencing all through high school and even into college. There was also a time when Lon had held court—as he often did—and recounted the singular exhilaration of that very first phone call with a girl. He had emphasized what a unique interchange it truly was. The first phone call, by its intrinsic nature, was something that could only happen once and never again. You couldn't have a second first phone call.

This had come up, weirdly enough, during his first phone call to Annie, in a setting galaxies removed from his days with Lon, Francis sneaking into the darkened bedroom, leaving Philip and Caleb to bicker over what to watch on TV that night. Annie herself had answered the phone, utterly crestfallen to hear from him. It was one of the most demoralizing few seconds of his life. Not even in his most grotesque imagination did he envision that her reaction would be unambiguous disappointment. But then suddenly Annie's tone changed dramatically. It happened, strangely enough, that she was acquainted with another Francis. That particular Francis was an overly friendly irritant in her sociology class, someone she had no desire to hear from.

His true identity now ascertained, the two were able to launch into a stunningly buoyant, far-ranging conversation of an hour's duration. At some point, as they were speaking, it dawned on him that this—now—was the official, unique first phone call, with all its attendant magic and exhilaration. Lon's observation, made all the way back during the wilds of eighth grade, had traveled through time to resonate here in Somerset Apartments on Witherspoon Avenue.

And here, at Tillman's Gulf, was Lon in the flesh, sitting in a car that had obviously seen better days, a hard-looking girl in the driver's seat. Lon seemed utterly astonished to find Francis working here, going so far as to open the door and step outside for closer scrutiny. *Francis*, he said with emphasis, but this was in no way a friendly salutation or expression of pleased surprise. It was exactly the opposite. "Francis *pumping gas*," Lon exclaimed, as if this was a revelation of the highest order. "I've been through some shitty times," he continued, the incredulity never leaving his voice. "But I ain't never had to pump gas!" He seemed genuinely stunned. And Francis couldn't help but notice the pure malice.

Lon tossed a quick, contemptuous glance at this girl in the driver's seat, who sat stock-still, gazing out the windshield. He had lost his license for a while, he told Francis. "Fucking Leedsville cops," Lon said, snorting, as if he was imparting common knowledge that needed no elaboration. "Dicks," he concluded emphatically. He stared at Francis anew, as if formulating some additional observations. Francis was again aware of this deep reservoir of scorn that Lon was emanating.

After the gas was dispensed and the car left the station, he was left to ponder if Lon had always harbored a deep-down resentment. There was a time when they had been such close, close friends. Perhaps Lon, all the while, had nurtured this secret hatred.

20

There had been a steady drumbeat of talk about the prostitution that had sprung up in Atlantic City. Like the hot-dog wars, this was another by-product of the casinos. It was said that Pacific Avenue, one of the main thoroughfares, was lined with them. Francis rarely, if ever, ventured forth into Atlantic City and he could find, now, no effective rationale for doing so. One night, setting out in his blue Chevette, he simply happened to drift along in that general direction.

The traffic, bound for Atlantic City, gradually grew denser, the drivers becoming slightly more abrasive. The hints of tawdriness, of hucksterism, began to make its appearance, anticipating the louche resort that lay just ahead. It was the polar opposite of the approach into Ocean City: crossing the bridge and glimpsing the exuberant, sun-splashed town of beaches and lemonade.

To his satisfaction, the prominent sign for Madame Carlotta, fortune-teller and palmist, was still intact, unchanged since his childhood, Madame Carlotta's name in big, bold letters and the oddball, crude symbols arranged in their haphazard format: an upturned palm, a crystal ball, a dollar sign. And then he wondered, as he had always wondered, who in the world would possibly avail themselves of Madame Carlotta's services.

He entered Atlantic City proper, shuddering inwardly, as usual, at the immediate appearance of the gruesome housing project on the right, which seemed more akin to a prison camp than someone's home, then carefully maneuvering around the thick traffic that swung around the rotunda of the war memorial. He navigated through the stop-and-start traffic, the traffic lights. The energetic jitneys, which halted over and over again to pick up and discharge passengers, were a constant impediment to the traffic flow, but he did finally wind up on the main artery of Pacific

Avenue. It did not take long to espy the presence of outlandishly costumed, freakish-looking women perched on one street corner after another. They were mostly black and seemed vaguely threatening, almost menacing, catering—he imagined—to a clientele of Mafioso or Barbarians. One, to Francis's intense mortification, caught his eye as his car crawled Pacific, motioning to him in a friendly greeting. Insulted, he resolutely stared in the other direction, as if his dignity had been besmirched, and sped up as much as the traffic would allow.

Some instinct, nonetheless, led him to a traffic spot blocks and blocks away—but not, for safety's sake, completely out of the way—thankfully avoiding the exorbitant parking lots and any interchange with an attendant.

And so here it was: Atlantic City at night.

His demeanor, Francis decided, would be of someone traversing Pacific Avenue without the slightest interest in anything remotely related to these nearly-nude women who would have sex with you at a moment's notice. What was required, though, to maintain this nonchalant demeanor? He pondered the implied requirements. Skulking about was ill-advised, of course—a dead giveaway. But a jaunty, not-a-care-in-the-world walk would be too overt: another sort of dead giveaway. He opted for a quiet look of subtle determination.

But as he began to traverse Pacific Avenue, that quiet look of subtle determination and his general composure quickly took a beating when the first jitney rolled by. The passengers could so easily include someone he was acquainted with, who would recognize him as he strolled not-so-innocently down Pacific Avenue. He wouldn't be fooling anybody and instinctively hid his face, looking down in shame.

A moment later, Francis almost jumped out of his skin as he was loudly hailed by an older, grizzled man who claimed to be a veteran in need of assistance. A short block later another man called out a greeting, lamenting that he had lost his wallet and needed just a few dollars to get home.

Pacific Avenue grew more crowded, the heavy traffic snaking past, jitneys zipping along. The cheap motels, neon flashing off and on, all seemed to be doing a brisk business. It was hard to shake the feeling that the entire avenue was aware of him, cognizant of what he was trying to do, passing judgment on his weak, lustful moral fiber.

Suddenly, a shockingly pleasant woman, entirely clad in garish red, approached in his direction. She smiled at him. Although her clothing was eye-catching, her makeup was much less extreme than the others. She was Caucasian, this woman, and he felt a current of anxiety for taking comfort in this: Perhaps it was latent racism on his part, but in this particular context—soliciting a prostitute—these worries seemed comically gratuitous. Her stomach, he could see now, was alluringly tanned and she was bedecked with jewelry. For this one brief moment there seemed to be nobody around. If he was to undertake this momentous leap into carnal debauchery, this was the time to do it. He tamped down an impulse of panic, trying to steady himself. The red-clad woman met his gaze and a surge of wild, uninhibited adventure shot through his body: This was really happening. She was now very close by and he realized suddenly that he had no idea of what the accepted protocol was. Now they were practically face-to-face; there was no time for further indecision. He blurted out his simple inquiry: "How much?"

This red-clad woman with the tanned stomach went through a rapid combination of facial expressions Francis had never seen before: a flit of a smile, a look of chagrin and embarrassment, all inflected with a strong measure of contempt. The woman, he could easily perceive now, was certainly no hooker; perhaps a tourist, a local bartender. His query as to how much now seemed loud and shrill, a piercing factory whistle. Seized with abject mortification, Francis darted quickly ahead, but was then jolted by the blaring of a car horn: In his haste, he had sauntered in front of a motel driveway, heedless of a car exiting into the street.

And so Francis walked aimlessly on for a few more minutes, eventually finding himself amid a cluster of desolate-looking businesses: a buyer and seller of gold, a pawnshop, and a venue that promised—in big, bold letters—sexy, live nude girls. And before he could talk himself out of it, he darted in.

The quiet, dark interior felt completely sequestered from the street outside. He'd somehow expected an immediate manifestation of these sexy, live nude girls—like a stage—but the sexy, live nude girls didn't seem at all in evidence. The place smelled of disinfectant and some artificial, chemical sweetness. Francis took a hurried look around. Three guys, he could see now, were off in a corner near the hallway, deep in a hushed discussion. He instinctively felt for his wallet.

A short, unkempt older black man suddenly materialized out of nowhere, standing alongside him, jocularly asking his name, as if Francis was at a party and being welcomed by the friendly host. "Chuck," he smoothly trotted out without a hint of hesitation, inwardly pleased that he was sufficiently cunning as to be able to instantaneously crank out an alias.

The older man smiled. "Well, Chuck," he began warmly. "It'll be ten bucks for the show. For twenty, she'll come around and see you in private." And then the older man chuckled; a warm, good-humored laugh.

But Francis didn't want to be touched; not at all, and this he declared without any pretense of dignity, then cursed his fecklessness. He had sounded squeaky, alarmist; not at all an adept man of the world who traveled with an alias. "You don't want to be touched?" the old man asked in a tone of complete disbelief, chuckling anew and shaking his head, as if he was forever amused by people's eccentricities.

And Francis—almost not of his volition, as if he were being compelled by some overpowering force—pulled out his wallet and handed this man ten dollars.

Those three men deep in conversation, whoever they were, were no longer apparent. And now Francis was directed down a dark corridor, his unease growing. There was a dungeon-like booth reserved for his use and he slipped in, shutting the door behind him.

He found himself staring at a thick pane of glass. And then suddenly the space beyond this glass was flooded with harsh white light. To his surprise, a stocky, bare-breasted, olive-complexioned woman in sparkly blue panties was sitting on a wooden stool. "What's your name, honey?" this woman called out, licking her lips suggestively. They certainly were big on names here. He answered instinctively that his name was Carl and then cursed himself. He was Chuck, not Carl. Now his cover was blown. "Hi Carl," this woman purred, licking her fingers and then running her hands over her nipples. "I'm Stardust," she said by way of introduction. "It's twenty bucks for the show, baby," she insisted smoothly. He hadn't been informed of this additional fee; these were not the prices quoted to him by the grubby older man who'd been so intent on learning his name. But bickering over this would be beyond ludicrous. He took out his wallet, momentarily confused as to how to offer the money. "In the slot, Carl," Stardust informed him, and, sure enough, a slot lay just to his right. Francis, now in the guise of Carl, slipped the twenty in.

Without preamble, Stardust turned around to display her ass, which she shook energetically and, for good measure, gave a few slaps. She turned around, jiggling her large breasts, flickering her tongue in and out as Francis remained stock-still, half transfixed, half mortified. "I'm a secret freak," Stardust declared out of nowhere, running her hands up and down her body. And then her demeanor changed. "Carl..." she said in almost a moan. "...you are one sexy guy." She shut her eyes and groaned. "One sexy guy," she declared again in what seemed to be an approximation of significant arousal. "Let me see your big cock," she continued, and now Stardust was rubbing her crotch, the shiny blue panties moving up and down, twisting around into her fingers. "Carl," she moaned again. "Yeah... fuck me with your big, hard cock." He tried to will himself into arousal, but the feelings that were percolating were the opposite of any sort of arousal.

"Carl," she moaned again, and in that same tone of near orgasm told him that for an extra forty dollars they could party. They could *really* party; they could party right here and now for only forty dollars.

And suddenly he'd had enough; feeling worse than a hapless college boy: embarrassed, repulsed, utterly at a loss as how to end this exchange. He simply left, opening the door to the booth and stepping out into the corridor, leaving—in full view—a near-naked, moaning woman licking her fingers and requesting an extra forty dollars.

He tried to depart with as much dignity as possible. A woman's voice was calling after someone; a few seconds later he realized that the name being uttered was "Carl." It was Stardust, imploring Carl to return. He'd forgotten his own alias. Then a wave of panic washed over him. In a few short seconds he would be exiting onto Pacific Avenue: well-traveled, crowded Pacific Avenue. Francis hadn't anticipated that he'd actually have to exit. He felt sick with impending shame. "Carl," he heard Stardust implore, and then there was a man's voice calling out to someone else as well. There was no choice but to brazen it out, depart through those doors and into the thick of Pacific Avenue at night, consequences be damned. The male voice called out again. *Chuck! Hey Chuck!* this voice was saying. Francis had again forgotten his first, earlier alias, and as he exited the building, he could hear the calls echoing throughout the interior: *Carl... Carl... Chuck! Hey, Chuck!*

This stretch of Pacific Avenue was, to his enormous relief, deserted. It took every bit of willpower not to break into a run on the long way back to his car. A block later he was hit up for money—again—by a mild-mannered sort who called him "sir" and begged for a moment of his time.

21

His informal tally of license plates continued: Tennessee, Ontario, Wisconsin. One driver had cleverly traversed the prohibition against using obscenities on personal plates, banking on the fact that nobody in authority would understand what a plate bearing the supposedly nonsensical *SCATOS* meant. But Francis knew: It was Greek for *shit*, a bit of knowledge imparted by that smutty guy of Greek descent from the dorms during sophomore year. He suddenly couldn't remember the name of that smutty guy, who had seemed just a little too taken with the homoerotic stereotypes of Greek culture, making constant, joking references to anal sex. Francis shot the *SCATOS* driver a knowing, you-can't-fool-me sort of look.

Then there were the bumper stickers: The endless political boosterism of local politics in far-flung states and locales—mayoral races, city-council elections, incomprehensible references to specific regional and local issues. Biblical verses. Homages to bands, musicians. *I'm not Fonda Hanoi Jane. South Jersey Statehood Now!*

Some of the cars would have the Phillies game on their radios, Joe following the incremental progress as the hours of the shift advanced, gleaning the highlights. Francis had discovered, to his amazement, that Joe actually worked another job, often putting in an additional eight-hour shift at some auto-supply store before beginning his stint at Tillman's. This was to be kept hidden, Joe requested, from Sonny, Dewey, Dutch, and especially Mr. Tillman. By doing this, he was able to pay off all his bills and even salt some money away at a fantastically speedy rate. He and the old lady, though, weren't getting along at all. They were thinking of calling it quits. Joe, not surprisingly, was suffering from an ulcer.

Sixteen hours of work a day. Francis had his own, brief taste of this sort of existence, when after an eleven-to-seven graveyard shift, he was required to return to work at three in the afternoon until eleven at night. In all probability, it had been a scheduling oversight on the part of Mr. Tillman. Sonny was sympathetic, but—in the end—not *that* sympathetic. "It's a twister, kid," he said with what passed as empathy. And so, when seven in the morning rolled around, Francis drove his weary, smudged self to Buzby's for coconut pancakes and half a pot of coffee, got home, showered, slept some, arose a scant four hours later, ate, and then journeyed back to the station for his three-to-eleven, feeling very proud and hardy, although this only happened once and he'd been forced to spend the next day recovering on the beach, much of it asleep on his towel.

This was something Joe must have experienced all the time and without letup. He also managed—ulcer and all—to somehow flesh out a life, he and his old lady going to Wildwood or out to dinner or to the movies with Norm and Norm's old lady. Francis began viewing Joe in an entirely new light: part superman, part freak of nature.

There were times during the day when, within the space of a few minutes, the incoming traffic would utterly evaporate, as if an edict had been issued that for a brief amount of time, Tillman's Gulf was required to transform into a large, sleepy station. There was no rhyme or reason to any of this. The crew would gather briefly in the threadbare office, Sonny occupying the creaky office chair that seemed as if it was strained to the breaking point by his great girth, stirring his coffee with the end of a pencil, lighting another cigarette and staring absently at the pumps. Dutch too availed himself of the opportunity for a cigarette, jovial and talkative, discussing a particularly irksome customer or obnoxious broad. Dutch and sometimes Dewey were the ones who imparted news from the greater world outside the station. A new restaurant, for example, had opened up right on Harbor Road, near where the old duck farm used to be. Big, substantial portions could be had for a reasonable sum: Roast beef, corn or fries, choice of vegetable, a large soda. Sonny usually remained silent during these recitations, occasionally tossing in a stray bit of information. What one of the troopers had said, a big repair job, snatches of information from the Garden House: That cocky nigger— the one who delivered bread—had finally quit for good.

Sonny was the one who would confirm that yes, Mr. Tillman was coming by during the afternoon, at which Dewey would look slightly bemused. Dutch would roll his eyes. And then Sonny would stub out the last of his cigarette, hoist himself up from the squeaky chair, and lumber off toward the back, Francis issuing a silent plea that Sonny was heading in any direction but the bathroom. If Sonny—or, for that matter, Mr. Tillman—sequestered themselves in the stall, a half hour would elapse before they'd emerge and the bathroom as a whole would be basically uninhabitable for a good hour after that, Francis resorting to running over to the Garden House and taking a piss in their facilities.

"I have nothing but respect for the man," Sonny would again insist shortly before Mr. Tillman's expected arrival. "But he's getting *senile*. He don't know what the fuck he's doing. Why doesn't he *just stay the fuck home?*" And then Sonny would shoot Francis a meaningful glance. "It's fucked-up, kid," came the expected conclusion. And then as Francis departed to resume his duties, Sonny would call out his logical afterthought: "It's all your fault, kid."

22

It was boredom, not lust, which was the catalyst for a return trip to Atlantic City, this time in the early afternoon. Traffic, even at this hour, was still thicker than he'd remembered in the past. And then Atlantic City loomed ahead, the new casinos poking up against the familiar skyline.

It was much easier, of course, to find a parking spot during the day, less of an effort to avoid the expensive commercial parking lots. Many of these lots now offered reimbursement in conjunction with the casinos. This was intended as an inducement, but to Francis the process seemed entirely too laborious, forcing one to trek deep into the bowels of the casino, parking stub in hand, locating the redemption center, and waiting in a long, annoying line for a parking-validation stamp, and then—whenever it was you exited the casino—presenting it to the parking-lot attendant.

He parked a few blocks away and was again solicited for money, this time by an overly friendly man who seemed visibly drunk. Francis was aware that prostitution was a nighttime, not a daytime, phenomenon, yet he found himself surreptitiously glancing around for any evidence that some of these women possibly plied their trade in the afternoon. There was not a hooker to be seen, of course, something he noted with equal measures of relief and disappointment.

These new casinos were soulless and imposing. Their emergence was, in addition, confusing. The Frontenac Hotel, for example, which had been such an integral part of Atlantic City, was now gone. The Frontenac had been a decrepit jewel, a once-grand hotel with pillars and elaborate turrets; an abundance of ornate, complicated architectural geegaws—this odd combination of stateliness and vulgarity. Back when he and Jeanette were little, they all ventured into the Frontenac for the sake of sheer curiosity. The memory of the shocking decrepitude was still vivid: The faded, almost ratty carpeting, the chipped staircase, the floors badly in need of scrubbing.

A few years before, the Frontenac had been demolished in a military-like operation in which the entire structure had been obliterated via a planned, spectacular implosion, the old hotel dramatically collapsing within a few seconds. Now, with all these changes to Atlantic City's terrain, he could no longer place the Frontenac's specific locale.

Francis ascended the boardwalk, bound for nowhere in particular. There was no gas to pump this day. And there were certainly no classes to attend, no papers to write, no studying. There was nowhere he needed to be.

Quite arbitrarily, he meandered into the lobby of the Goldmine Casino. A gigantic cage stretched from floor to ceiling, packed with mechanical, colorful birds in garish plumages of yellows, reds, purples. These birds, Francis recalled, had become something of a celebrated thing. Every few minutes they came to life, singing songs and telling jokes, and right on cue flashing red and yellow lights emanated from the cage, punctuated by a loud, brassy fanfare of prerecorded music. Feeling somewhat foolish, he gravitated toward the cage. The music swelled to a crescendo and now the ersatz birds began singing. With surprising rapidity, a crowd had materialized around the cage and now Francis found himself amid a large group of gamblers and tourists.

Each bird took a brief turn. A yellow parrot, straw hat perched at a jaunty angle, commenced with a Jimmy Durante routine. The next bird—a pink and purple figure of uncertain lineage—sounded like Elvis; the one after, Francis realized, was Wayne Newton. The crowd reveled in this, the birds' song and patter, laughing uproariously, even applauding. A drunk and warbling Dean Martin was followed by a green bird that departed from the strictly musical format, executing a Johnny Carson imitation that Francis had to admit was pitch-perfect. The crowd laughed anew. He moved on to the casino floor.

The interior of the Goldmine Casino was a realm all its own, row after row of slot machines bracing the floor, a steady current of beeps and buzzes, flashing lights, and he wandered through row after identical row, akin to an assembly line, nearly every slot machine commandeered by a grim, serious-looking gambler—many of them older—unsmiling and somberly absorbed in their labors, feeding quarter after quarter into the machines: An endless stream of coinage. And with a whoosh and a clatter, the slot machine would occasionally reward the gambler's efforts by regurgitating some of the quarters, the players depositing their money back into the slot machines. Art had heard that some of these fanatical slot enthusiasts—so convinced that their chance at beating the odds depended on their particular slot machine and so unwilling to budge—had actually pissed their pants rather than relinquish their position.

The casino provided large plastic tubs—akin to popcorn containers at the movies—prominently emblazoned with the Goldmine's puke-gold logo. These tubs were absolutely everywhere: piles and piles of them on the slot machines, stacked up against the walls, by the bathrooms. Wherever you were, you could scoop up your winnings at a moment's notice.

He was seized by the spirit of adventure and looked around for a two-dollar blackjack table. If he was finally going to attempt playing blackjack, a two-dollar minimum would most likely be his speed, but these two-dollar tables did not seem to be in evidence here at the Goldmine. He waded through the casino floor in search, now, of a five-dollar table, the hubbub of the crowd gradually increasing, and finally he came across the cluster of five-dollar tables.

The dealer at the nearest table had departed. Amid much hullabaloo, a new dealer—a middle-aged woman—assumed the helm and said something that Francis was unable to ascertain. Yet it must have been funny, whatever it was this middle-aged woman had said. The card players, perched on their seats and hemmed in at the table, began to laugh. Small knots of people, scattered throughout the casino, seemed to be perpetually in the midst of hurried consultations: security guards, pit bosses, management types, other dealers. The provocatively attired waitresses weaved back and forth, trays laden down with exotic, complicated drinks. From somewhere across the casino floor he could hear the strains of excited shouts, cheering.

The blackjack table nearest to him was packed so full that Francis began to think his chance would never come, but suddenly an available seat opened up and with a mixture of curiosity and trepidation, he took his place, proffering a twenty-dollar bill to the pleasant dealer who had made everyone laugh and receiving his puny little stake of four chips.

There were no clocks at the Goldmine Casino, no windows; no delineation between night and day. The dealer dealt everyone their allotted cards. A dull-looking man in a suit, reeking of metallic-smelling aftershave, was wedged into Francis's right; a heavy-set, dour-looking older woman was seated to his left. From time to time he'd heard discussions of complicated blackjack strategy: when to stay, when not to stay; the house's advantage, doubling down. None of it made even the least bit of sense, but sitting here now he wished he'd paid a modicum of attention. He tried hard to make it look as if he knew what he was doing, affecting a blasé mien as he—per custom—tapped the dark-purple tablecloth to indicate his desire for another card, or authoritatively sliced the air with his right hand to indicate that no further cards were required.

Another cheer could be heard from the far reaches of the Goldmine. Craps, Francis guessed. Craps—the little he knew about it—was interactive, the crowd often given to vociferously voicing its feelings. To his mild disgust, his arm brushed against the fat arm of the dour older woman sitting next to him. And then faster than he thought possible, he lost four bets in a row and his twenty dollars was gone. Now he was forced, feeling vaguely foolish, to vacate his seat. He tried not to consider what those twenty dollars could have purchased.

Uncertain as what to do next, he ambled his way over to the dark casino lounge, sinking into one of the well-cushioned seats. The lounge, at this time of day, was almost entirely deserted, save for a much older, resplendently fashioned man with a roguish moustache who was sitting up front at the bar, wearing a blue suit with cuff links that glistened to such an extent that Francis could make them out from where he was sitting. The old man was nursing an elaborate drink. Francis felt a pang of unease. What, exactly, was the protocol for ordering drinks in a casino lounge?

A smiling waitress in a skimpy uniform loomed over him, handing him an extensive drinks menu and a bowl of peanuts, which Francis—happy to come across something familiar in this foreign land of the casino lounge—began consuming immediately. The mammoth list of drinks seemed as complicated as blackjack strategy and he was suddenly, painfully aware of how easy it would be to look like an utter rube in front of this alluring, sophisticated waitress. Upon her return, he ordered a Rolling Rock, which seemed like a fail-safe option: Nobody laughed at beer. But when the cold bottle and tall, skinny glass were set before him, his enthusiasm faded quickly. A Rolling Rock was really the last thing he wanted now.

He took some obligatory swallows and consumed most of the remaining peanuts, but the beer made him feel slightly sluggish. The older man at the bar, he noticed now, had been joined by a very tanned younger woman in fancy dress, the sort of woman who would be in attendance at a sophisticated party with soft music, hors d'oeuvres, and cocktails. It appeared introductions were being offered, the woman smiling, both she and the old man shaking hands. Francis turned his attention back to his beer. The waitress refilled the peanut bowl. When he glanced back at the bar, the old man and woman were toasting each other.

With a nagging sense of obligation, he finished most of the beer and then asked for the check, which was promptly offered and predictably exorbitant. The waitress, done with him, offered only the most perfunctory of good-byes. It had begun to dawn on him what was transpiring up at the bar. The old man and younger woman departed.

Back out on the casino floor, Francis was startled by the appearance of a scruffy, bearded oddball in threadbare clothes. And then he was startled all the more as a phalanx of four beefy security guards materialized out of nowhere, converging on this man in a perfectly executed formation and—as one—actually lifting him into the air like a human battering ram and charging through a side exit. All of this, incredibly, had transpired in almost complete silence. Within a minute there was no evidence whatsoever that this had even taken place at all, the casino going back to its usual buzzes, its beeping.

23.

He was, he suddenly realized, very hungry and had had enough of the Goldmine Casino. There was a brief moment of disorientation upon reemerging into the boardwalk's light of day. Right across from the Goldmine was another new attraction, the mammoth Atlantic One Mall, shaped like an ocean liner.

To Francis's own surprise, he was suddenly filled with a deeply felt, almost painful yearning for the old, somewhat tawdry Atlantic City: the Steel Pier—where the fifth grade had gone for a class trip and a gang of black toughs had swooped down and stolen a dollar right out of his hand—Nathan's Hot Dogs, the Frontenac Hotel, the long-shuttered burlesque hall, and even those annoying bicycle surreys that leisurely transported tourists up and down the boardwalk. All of these were gone, including the requisite contingent of rough-featured, slightly unkempt old men in uncomfortable-looking polyester slacks, puffing away on large, odiferous cigars. There had always been an unofficial quota of these old men and their odiferous cigars, who were positioned strategically at regular intervals up and down the boardwalk. It was as if the equilibrium of Atlantic City depended on these old men. Where had they gone?

And these feelings puzzled him, this desperate yearning for a place that had, after all, never really loomed large in his life, had never been all *that* important to him.

The Atlantic One Mall had a record store and a magazine shop, but from what he could glean it seemed mostly full of uninspiring clothing stores and a few food dispensaries: an ice cream parlor, a strudel takeout stand. He had never given strudel any thought whatsoever, but here was a business that trafficked in it exclusively.

The mere existence of the Atlantic One Mall was slightly discombobulating. Malls were in no way the province of Atlantic City; there was the Creslea Mall—

simply *the mall*, of course—where so many of them congregated, spending all that useless time browsing through the bins at Shoresounds, snagging the free mints and cheese spread at Buckeye Hills, purchasing a slice of pizza at Angel's. That was *the mall*, the one and only mall: an ordered, fixed part of the universe. This Atlantic One Mall was another matter entirely.

The real eating to be done here was on the second-floor food court, which at least was making an attempt—however ineptly—to be international, boasting Chinese, Indian, Mexican food. And off to the side was an actual Nathan's Hot Dogs. In this new Atlantic City, Nathan's Hot Dogs was apparently deemed too déclassé to keep its prominent perch on the boardwalk. It now had be gussied up and sequestered here in a food court.

After a moment of deliberation, he chose the Indian eatery, which seemed to be actually managed and operated by Indians, quickly settling on tandoori chicken and a Coke, and then taking a seat at a nearby table. There were a few other customers at scattered tables, various food scents battling it out here at the food court: The odors of Chinese contesting with Indian, Mexican clashing with Nathan's. The Coke, unfortunately, was watered down with too much ice; the tandoori chicken surprisingly messy, requiring the assistance of an endless amount of napkins. Francis felt, all of a sudden, drenched in ridiculousness, a laughable little figure with a weird strip of calloused skin on his hand, stack of napkins piling up beside him. He finished eating and quickly made for the stairs.

Right near the exit he spotted a small, incredibly compact coffee emporium that he had missed upon entering the Atlantic One Mall. There was not one wasted inch: overflowing sacks of glistening beans ringing the entrance and crammed inside the tiny shop. The smell was hypnotic. His taste in coffee had been affirmatively rotgut, a means to an end: something to be imbibed during finals week or when a term paper was due; a method to push him through the long hours at Tillman's.

These stacks of coffee were intoxicating. A girl roughly his own age had materialized, also intent at perusing the cornucopia. But in sharp contrast to his provincialism, she displaying an air of expertise he himself woefully lacked. She had lots of hair, this girl; masses of curly blond hair cascading down almost to her shoulders. They met each other's gaze and smiled.

"When I can't decide what I want," she began without preamble, "I take a bean from the sack and chew it." And she proceeded to do just that, deftly picking off a bean and popping it into her mouth. "Try it," she urged, and Francis, startled and curious both, did just that. It wasn't an altogether unpleasant experience, the intense bitterness of the coffee bean offset by a smoky, cinnamon-like flavor, a satisfying crunch.

And so they began chatting here in front of these massive sacks of coffee beans. There was something about her—the idiosyncratic tasting of the bean, the feeling that she had emerged out of thin air—that made Francis certain that this girl was from somewhere else. It was just the opposite. She was a local, and not just a local, but a graduate of Kittahicken High School, Leedsville High's archrival—although almost nothing had been more ludicrous to him than that inane Leedsville-Kittahicken antagonism.

Her name was Liz and they chatted some more. She and a few friends, Liz mentioned matter-of-factly, were going to the Sunspot this very night to hear the Jetsons. Francis, of course, was well acquainted with the Sunspot, the Margate bar perched right near Lucy the Elephant and the beach. The Sunspot's locale rendered it a popular watering hole after a day in the sun.

The Jetsons were an atrocious two-person band made up of an old married couple. Their sub-par music had accompanied many a beer-soaked afternoon at the Sunspot.

Would he like to join them tonight? she inquired. And Francis, feeling bold and off-kilter at the same time, agreed to join this Liz and her friends before he had a chance to talk himself out of it.

24

Leedsville cranked by his window as he began the drive toward Margate. Hitchhikers, he had come to gradually realize, had inexplicably vanished from the terrain. It had been such a constant in his life, all of them so blithely unaware of the potential threat to personal safety as they thumbed their way to and from the beach. Common sense, apparently, had finally won the day and thumbing rides seemed to have gone basically extinct.

Francis himself had kept up the practice during that first year of college, thumbing the occasional ride back and forth. He and Caleb were hitchhiking back from some party and two older guys had picked them up. Something had seemed wrong from the start, the driver and his friend both beefy and impassive, eyes glazed. It soon became apparent they had no intention whatsoever of stopping the car, driving on and on, heedless of Caleb and Francis's protestations. The intent, apparently, had been merely to fuck with them, to scare the shit out of two hitchhikers. That had been more than accomplished—it had really and truly been very frightening. Finally, when the endeavor had lost its novelty, he and Caleb were allowed to squeeze their way out of the back, plunked down in the middle of nowhere, while the car roared off into the night.

They were now miles from University Avenue and the dorms. Hours later, as they finally trudged their exhausted way through town, they came upon that very same car in a parking lot. He and Caleb stood, thunderstruck, and gaped. That it was the same car was beyond dispute. There was no way to forget the distinctive puke-orange exterior, the jagged crack in the back window, the shiny bolt of duct tape affixed to the front passenger seat. They'd had plenty of time, during their captivity, to stare straight ahead, eyes focused on the duct tape while they wondered what fate had in store.

Even now—driving en route to Margate and the Sunspot—the recollection of what he and Caleb had done next made him intensely uncomfortable. Francis had unzipped his fly, letting loose a torrent of yellow piss that splattered all over the car's side doors. Caleb had also set to work, crouching down and letting the air out of the back tires, taking great care to avoid Francis's urine.

What they'd really done was taken complete leave of their senses. He and Caleb could have easily been discovered. Those two older guys had not been undertaking a friendly prank: They were malevolent. These were not college high jinks. Francis and Caleb's retaliation was just that: It was serious retaliation. The potential consequences, had they been discovered—and they certainly could have been discovered—would have been severe. They had opened themselves up to the prospect of extreme physical harm. He and Caleb could have gotten hurt. Very, very hurt.

He drove on Mariner Road for a good fifteen minutes until the intersection. To the left led the way into the beginning of Creslea Road; to the right led to Margate. Within a minute or two, the briny, pungent odor of the marshes filled the air, permeating his car. There was a slight breeze; the marshland's spiky-green expanse fluttering in the wind.

Francis paid the toll on the small bridge that led into town, something that never failed to slightly annoy him; the nagging inconvenience of it all. Margate was compressed; shops and houses squashed together in row after continuous row, but it was a cheery sort of compactness: boutiques, clothing shops, doctors' offices, a florist.

Lucy the Elephant loomed off in the distance. Traffic, at times, could get as thick around here as that of Atlantic City, what with the Sunspot and Skeeter Boss's club a few blocks down. Parking was often an issue, but suddenly—providentially—a car pulled out of a space right in front of him.

There were nights here when the frenetic crush rivaled that of Bay Street, hordes of people filling up the sidewalks, the slow-moving cars maneuvering for any available spot: long, celebratory summer nights. It was less honky-tonk than Bay Street, for sure—or less honky-tonk than what Bay Street *had* been, what with the demise of Toby Hunt's. Tonight, though, things seemed more sedate. The odor of fries, meat, something sugary—that particular olfactory mélange that only existed by the beach—gently wafted over to him.

He tried not to look too confused as he entered the Sunspot and attempted to figure out where this Liz person was, but within seconds they had spotted each other, Liz perched at the bar with two girls—who Francis assumed were the friends she had mentioned—positioned on her left. She greeted him with an unexpectedly huge smile as he took a seat to her right. The various introductions were lost amid the noise and babble: the loud jukebox, the boisterous crowd. Liz seemed like a different person in this context, now done up in a bright, cheerful sundress and smelling enticingly of a citrus-like perfume; not at all like that mysterious figure who had materialized amid the coffee sacks of the Atlantic One Mall. Her hair, though, was as he remembered it: long, cascading; so blond it looked almost glowing.

These two friends had also gone to Kittahicken. There was a brief, eager back-and-forth on who knew who. He strained to remember people potentially in common. There was that guy at Angel's Pizza who'd gone to Kittahicken. Francis had once given him a ride from the mall to Leedsville; they'd pulled into the old lumberyard and gotten high. But the Sunspot's steady cacophony made further conversation difficult.

A good portion of the din was being generated by the four older guys at the table behind them. They were astonishingly loud, the conversation revolving almost exclusively around food: crab cakes and pizza, in particular, each participant outdoing the other in boisterous, exuberant attention to detail—sauces, preparation, portions. They knew some of the cooks by name. Liz, he could see, was nursing a gin and tonic. This wasn't a casino lounge, of course, with its confusing myriad of mixed drinks. Here, at the Sunspot, Francis was on safe ground. He could order whatever he wanted with the assurance that he would be making the correct choice. Proudly and affirmatively, he requested a Rolling Rock.

For want of something to say, he mentioned to Liz that he was trying to work off his shoobie tan, then instantly regretted his words. This might require an explanation of how he had been saddled with a shoobie tan in the first place. It was, of course, the tan of someone who pumped gas at Tillman's Gulf. He tried not to glance at his calloused right hand.

A drunk-looking trio at the table on the other side of the bar ordered another round. Liz, thankfully disinclined to probe too deeply into the origin of his shoobie tan, launched into an account of her own particular tanning difficulties, burdened as she was by this ultra-fair complexion, forced to be very aware of potential sunburn.

For reasons he couldn't ascertain, Liz appeared older and more worldly than he was. He made an effort not to glance at her breasts, which seemed large. His only true exposure to large breasts had been via that unfortunate incident with Punch.

To his own surprise, he felt grateful for the din, which spared the need for any additional forced banter. He was nominally adept at forced banter, but forced banter took the form of the ins and outs of one's major, roommate woes, living arrangements. And none of that was applicable now. He would have to cast about for new forced banter.

The Sunspot, all in all, had not been one of his most familiar haunts. Francis's allegiance had stayed mostly with Toby Hunt's and the familiar grime of Bay Street. And then there had been the Quay, the decrepit old bar on the other side of the Point. Local legend had it that the Quay served underage without even a perfunctory interest in adhering to the legal drinking age. And so, when he was seventeen, he and a few others—Art, Paul, Corky—had boldly approached the Quay, its bright red Budweiser sign shining like a beacon, braved the imposing front door, and with a bravado Francis hadn't felt in the least, entered the dimly-lit interior and took their seats at the bar.

This had all been Corky's doing. He had successfully entered the Quay a week before, informing one and all that yes, he'd been served without a hitch. Now Francis tried to unobtrusively follow Corky's lead, the confident, almost strutting, manner. Francis's trepidation evaporated quickly. It was true what everyone said about the Quay. The hatchet-faced older bartender didn't give a shit at all as to how old they were.

The plucky gang settled onto the tottering red barstools, ordering beer after beer, partaking of the spicy Slim Jims, staring out at the array of vintage Phillies memorabilia that packed the walls. Someone had actually taken the time and effort to craft a painting of Harry Kalas, the dulcet voice of the Phillies, and it hung—like a religious icon—in a position of prominence over the bar, watching over the Quay and all who drank here. An old man sat at the end of the bar in what seemed to be his regular perch. He was loudly expounding to the impassive bartender: The old man's uncle had been a big shot in Port Franklin. In fact, his uncle had *run* Port Franklin. His word was law.

When he said *jump*, every nigger in Port Franklin was forced to jump.

The Quay, subsequently, became their first watering hole. Soon, though, its appeal lessened, the novelty wearing off. Toby Hunt's and Bay Street at large soon beckoned. The Quay was forgotten.

And the Jetsons were an improbable phenomenon that had manifested itself fairly recently, while Francis had been away at school. They were the most incongruous musical attraction, an older husband and wife without any discernible musical talent, grinding out one horrible song after another, a hodgepodge of genres and styles: Perry Como upon Elvis upon a polka.

A consensus had emerged among the loud foursome at the table behind them. The Brigantine Pub, it was felt, was the winner when it came to crab cakes.

Mussels too. You could get a huge plate of crab cakes at the Brigantine Pub, piled yea high on one's plate. The focus of the conversation, then, shifted away from crab cakes, pizza, mussels. They were now dissecting the exploits of someone named Buzzy. Buzzy, apparently, had a ramshackle boat that he'd constructed all by himself. Its seaworthiness was debatable. You could always count on Buzzy for a ready quip on any occasion; some of his more famous bons mots were brought up, engendering bursts of thunderous laughter. A toast was offered up to Buzzy. Liz ordered another gin and tonic.

An older man, hair greased back in a militantly old-fashioned mode, face expressionless, glided over to the jukebox and yanked its heavy black cord out of the wall socket. The music wilted away and died within seconds. It was Mr. Jetson, the crowd realized, and word quickly spread throughout the Sunspot.

Francis hadn't known the origin of the Jetson name, if it was a play on their real last name or a complete concoction, but whatever the derivation, here they were:

Mr. Jetson setting up a little drum kit and Mrs. Jetson—equally old, equally impassive—busying herself with a tiny keyboard. Within moments, they were ready.

Their first song began without any preamble. Mrs. Jetson's sprightly keyboard playing was competent enough, but Mr. Jetson's off-kilter drumming began to drown out her efforts. His drum solos were the stuff of legend: loud, long, and utterly formless, pounding away while the packed daytime crowd whooped and hollered. Tonight, though, he was somewhat more sedate.

Conversation was nearly impossible. Francis ordered another Rolling Rock. The Jetsons had begun—from what he could piece together—"Danke Schoen," and now it was Mrs. Jetson's turn to wander into musical incoherence, soon augmented—again—by Mr. Jetson's bombs-away drum solo.

Suddenly Francis was gripped by an overwhelming sorrow. The Jetsons were here to be laughed at, pure and simple. They were a spectacle, too old or inept or indifferent to the fact that they were a target of mockery. It all seemed unspeakably, horribly cruel. He remembered an encounter at Tillman's from a few days past: A man not entirely dissimilar-looking to Mr. Jetson had gotten out of his car in, of all things, a Fonzie T-shirt. The rendering of Fonzie was crude, barely recognizable; almost as if a kid had sketched the whole thing out. Printed over the amateurish design was *H-e-e-e-y I'm the Fonz!* This man too was a spectacle, going about his day-to-day routine utterly unaware of how shockingly ridiculous this Fonzie T-shirt looked. Francis felt wretched; wretched for the man in the Fonzie T-shirt, wretched for the Jetsons, and—for good measure—wretched for himself. The cruel, heartless world was full of innocent targets, stripping them of any human dignity and making a mockery of their very existence.

Francis looked around the Sunspot, eventually meeting Liz's eyes; the two smiled at each other. Memories

99

of the Harmony Lounge floated in front of him: the crush of students, the pitchers of beer, the bands. One night he had staggered out, very inebriated, to witness a fight in progress between a beefy, T-shirted frat-boy type and a tall, skinny New Wave sort, neither of whom Francis recognized. The frat boy was being bodily restrained, bellowing loudly that he was going to tear his adversary's fucking head off. The New Wave guy, hands up in supplication and skinny black tie impeccably arranged, earnestly expressed his aversion to any sort of conflict, and then suddenly landed a solid punch on the frat boy's head. This brought on another spate of bellowing invective. The frat boy's opponent, again declaring his pacific intentions, managed to land another solid punch, bringing on another wave of loud threats and verbal commotion. This might have gone on all night.

Francis was suddenly weary of the Sunspot. Liz also seemed fatigued. Even the table behind them, having exhausted their treasure trove of Buzzy lore, had quieted down.

He and Liz exited together, leaving her Kittahicken friends—whose names he had finally managed to catch and then had immediately forgotten—ensconced at the bar.

The warm night air was quieter now, almost still. A few cars passed by; he could hear a burst of loud, brassy music coming from Skeeter Boss's. The air smelled faintly of cooking. Then he was slightly jolted as Liz asked him—outright—if he wanted to spend a day with her at Oonamee Lake out in Haslams Landing. This was disorienting on a number of levels. He hadn't really expected that Liz actually existed outside of this one, specific day. They had met in unexpected circumstances at the Atlantic One Mall and then, equally unexpectedly, had arranged to meet at the Sunspot. For some reason, it didn't seem like there would be additional contact. And now there would be.

And until this moment he hadn't really considered the possibility of actually venturing to Oonamee Lake. He'd grown up with it, of course, heard it mentioned, driven past it once or twice. But had never actually *gone*. His fixed frame of reference was limited to the beaches and ocean. It didn't include a lake.

But most of all, he realized again, he was in thoroughly unexplored terrain. Courtship—if that's indeed what this was—was full of elaborate, interconnected events. Most of that interconnectedness transpired in delineated settings: the library, classrooms, eateries, dorms, student domiciles, the Harmony, University Avenue. Those settings, though, had disappeared.

The only thing that did seem certain was that in a few days hence he would be meeting this Liz, who had materialized out of nowhere. They would be going to Oonamee Lake, a place both vaguely familiar and vaguely unfamiliar, which perfectly matched the circumstances of his life: vaguely familiar, vaguely unfamiliar.

PART 2

25

The house had been empty this morning. Francis had utilized this stretch of privacy to yet again play *Pomp and Circumstance*, unconsciously following along with the cadences of the piece: Lining up with his fellow graduates, all of them taking their positions, that brief moment in front of the crowd, receiving his degree with grace and dignity.

He settled in for the long ride to Haslams Landing, proceeding along Mariner Road and then to Creslea and its continuous stretch: the movie theater, McDonald's, the old Burger Chef—still vacant—Pantry Pride, and Traymore Furniture, possibly the single dullest store in human existence. There'd been a tiny head shop tucked away in one of the mini-plazas that dotted Creslea Road, unobtrusively perched near a real-estate office and an appliance store, crammed full with bongs, pipes, and all matter of paraphernalia. This head shop, Francis knew, had closed some time back.

And then came the Creslea Mall, which was not his focus today, of course, and he proceeded further along Creslea Road, passing the citadel-like Ocean Heights Liquors, a place of such nasty, intimidating repute that none of them—even after braving the Quay, even after having attained legal drinking status—had ever been tempted to venture forth inside.

Creslea Road fed into the Dray Horse Pike. Here he could drive faster. The buildings on the Pike were smaller, less in number: bait-and-tackle shop, ammo store, fresh corn for sale. The little, faded motels—cottages, really; just this side of decrepit—still dotted the Pike up and down. Within ten minutes one could glimpse the turrets and colorful banners of Storytime Hamlet, with its enticements of wandering through the twisty paths and jumbo replicas of Peter, Peter, Pumpkin Eater and his unfortunate wife, forever consigned to a life of misery inside a pumpkin shell;

the Little Old Lady Who Lived in a Shoe, along with her large, unruly brood; Snow White and the Seven Dwarfs, and so many others, all of which had so captivated him and Jeanette when they were little.

The radio today proved to be a disappointing source of entertainment. Kirby McAdoo commenced with a boring, unlistenable jag: A rival minister and his church had committed some sort of unpardonable sin. Out of loyalty to Jeanette, he made himself listen to the Rockin' Wave, hoping to hear the Kicks or Toohey's commercial. These were not forthcoming, but to his satisfaction FM 96 was embarking on yet another Big Kahuna Weekend; he'd heard Jeanette discussing some of the details. Finally he dispensed with the radio altogether.

He exited the Dray Horse Pike via the little traffic circle that connected to Route 49. And his was the only car, not surprisingly, traversing this circle plopped in the middle of nowhere, a traffic circle that seemed to serve no real purpose; enjoying the brief novelty of accelerating to his heart's content, barreling through a traffic circle heedless of any incoming cars.

For a few minutes he was trapped behind an old, ramshackle bus that was wheezing fumes. When it pulled off Route 49 he could see that it was filled with Mexican-looking men and women, obviously farmworkers. Glimpses could be seen of colorful, foreign fabric.

After that bus, Route 49 was basically his and his alone. He had forgotten how rural south Jersey could be. The Toulon Winery was off to the right, the huge edifice of a wine bottle towering over its entrance. The winery, though, after a series of financial fits and starts, had closed for good a few months back, the giant wine bottle an oddball, mute witness to what had been and was no longer.

Both sides of Route 49 were lined by pine trees, broken up at semi-regular intervals by farm stands, a beauty shop, a fancy-looking restaurant, an ice-cream shack. And then, on the left, was Fratarcangelli's U-pick-it blueberry farm. Around the time when Francis was in ninth or tenth grade, his mother and one of their neighbors, Mrs. O'Rourke, had spent the day there. He remembered her returning to the house that afternoon laden down with a massive amount of blueberries. It remained an eternal mystery to him, though, why anyone would voluntarily subject themselves to the rigors of spending a hot day performing the arduous task of blueberry-picking.

He was nearing Haslams Landing, approaching the diner and that huge art-deco gas station with its sparkling metallic glow, both of which he vaguely remembered. The Chevette's gas gauge was tilting toward the low end of things. On an impulse, he pulled into the station and one of its empty lanes, enjoying the novelty of being a gas-station customer and not an employee.

He was greeted by an older, courtly-looking attendant, wearing—of all things—white gloves, who then proceeded to inquire—in a distinct, unidentifiable foreign accent—if he could help him. This man with the white gloves quickly washed the Chevette's windows, filled the tank, and courteously took his money while Francis tried not to stare. Who was this accented, white-gloved attendant from another land? It all seemed somewhat mysterious. Perhaps Sonny or Dewey or Dutch would have inside information.

Route 49 continued on for a few more minutes: another, smaller U-pick-it, a grocery store, a used-car lot. And then Francis was in Haslams Landing. He needed to slow the car down considerably along the town's main drag, recognizing the imposing, pillared white courthouse that dominated the block. The essence of Haslams Landing in its entirety was laid out in front of him, its row of shops and offices: insurance, drugstore, fabric shop, old-fashioned candy store. At the end of the block was a satellite bureau of the *Atlantic City Journal-Bulletin*.

And then the main street ended as quickly as it had begun. He turned right, passing tree-lined blocks of older, formidable-looking houses, all of them impeccably maintained; most of them boasting expansive front porches and abundant lawns and gardens. A few of the houses seemed to date from colonial times. He turned right at the end of the neighborhood, a gigantic weeping willow in the last yard, so huge it almost seemed ready to burst its confines and take over the entire street itself.

Perhaps, he mused now, he would marry that tough-looking Garden House cashier. They'd live in a cozy house here in Haslams Landing, sitting on their equally cozy porch, drinking lemonade. He'd get a job at the *Journal-Bulletin*; his wife would work in a gift shop or store. Or maybe their domicile would be in the Point. You could walk to some of the restaurants in the Point, or drive to the diner for a meal of chop steak and a baked potato. For fun, he and his wife—that tough-looking Garden House cashier— would go blueberry picking or play cards with their neighbors. College, Annie—his entire life up north—would fade into hazy irrelevance. *Pomp and Circumstance* would cease to have any meaning for him whatsoever.

The shimmering of Oonamee Lake could be observed as soon as he made the right turn. In less than a minute he was pulling into its small parking lot, the closing of his car door sounding surprisingly loud to his own ears in this tranquil setting. And there was Liz. True to her account of her light-complexioned travails, she was covered up with longish shorts and a flowing pink shirt with a hood hanging from the back. She looked vaguely silly, he had to admit. She seemed to have just arrived, in the last stages of setting out her beach towel, arranging her things. Francis, unwittingly, paused for a moment, briefly unsure of how to proceed. Oonamee Lake was the direct opposite of the crowded beaches of Ocean City or Margate, where you could slip in relatively unobtrusively.

Now Liz turned to him and waved hello. He hadn't anticipated the fact that he was, in essence, making a grand entrance onto Oonamee Lake. And yet he couldn't simply stand here, pondering how to proceed. He had no choice but to approach.

"Give me a kiss," Liz said cheerfully, nonchalantly, but there was nothing coquettish or come-hither in this, more along the lines of a friendly, slightly eccentric request, and after the brief kiss he placed his towel next to hers, stealing surreptitious glances. There was a slight element of physical formidability to Liz in ways that he couldn't articulate.

The lake, in contrast to the beach, felt cramped and confined. There was an unexpected feeling of conspicuousness—no sand to sink into, no surf or waves to provide an aural backdrop. Oonamee Lake was still, quiet.

To the right of the lake was an enormous white gazebo, which seemed well-maintained and thoroughly functional, no doubt used for concerts in which masses of old people set out their lawn chairs to listen to wholesome music, perhaps of the type Larry Veniero played. And when Francis settled here in Haslams Landing and took his job at the newspaper—turning his back on the rest of the world— perhaps this is where he would come regularly, to these concerts by the lake.

His shoobie tan, he noted with satisfaction, had mostly disappeared, a testament to his perseverance and stick-to-itiveness. Here was goal he had set; here was a tangible accomplishment. An older couple was perched in back of them, up on a little elevated portion to Francis and Liz's left, near a clump of trees. From here, he and Liz could hear snatches of their conversation, bursts of elderly laughter.

There were no radios in earshot, no steady engine drones of those rattling biplanes flying overhead with their advertising banners. And, of course, there was no boardwalk.

What was there to do, ultimately, at this lake? Francis mused out loud if people went boating here. It was as if Liz had been waiting for just this sort of inquiry. Her face broke into a wide smile, happy to provide a detailed answer: A family friend knew someone on the Haslams Landing town council. And the boating policy was a definitive, emphatic *no*. This part of Oonamee Lake was absolutely off-limits to any boating whatsoever. And then she continued her explanation: The lake, further up, widened considerably. The water deepened. There were docks. Boating and even water-skiing were permitted.

He hadn't known any of this. Once and only once had he ever gone water-skiing. Corky's cousin had use of a boat and they had all gone out on the bay. Francis's actual time up on the water skis had been around three seconds before he was unceremoniously pitched into the water. In retrospect, the whole thing—the boat, the water-skiing—had probably been illegal. It was a wonder all of them had escaped the attention of the police or even serious injury.

The day was warm, verging on muggy. Chunks of large white clouds drifted across the sky. There was an unexpected burst of loud conversation and Francis and Liz—startled—both turned their heads. That older couple had left the lake, now replaced by a new, larger batch of elderly people; an entire contingent, as if Oonamee Lake had strict time limits for old people: one group out, one group in. This new infusion were not just greater in number, but a good deal more boisterous and energetic, the men and women settling in for the long haul, arranging their chairs and then attending to an extensive array of newspapers, food, paperbacks, towels, lotion. One of them, a corpulent, very old woman, energetically tottered down to the water's edge, giving Francis and Liz a hearty, enthusiastic wave, and then hollered something about the weather.

Liz had been to the lake, off and on, as a child. These had been bucolic interludes with her siblings and parents. It was before the divorce, before all of it. She hinted strongly of familial conflict on a grand scale, bonds ripped permanently asunder. There was a noticeable tone that indicated no wish to expand on any of this. She seemed genuinely, uncommonly eager to hear stories of his parents, his upbringing; especially curious about the details of Jeanette's life, her school, her work at FM 96.

Liz seemed to Francis to be a combination of stints. She had done a stint at the community college. She'd had a stint living in Cherry Hill, a stint working as a bookkeeper in her father's office. Most amazing of all was a stint living in back of Storytime Hamlet. He'd been dimly aware that there was a cluster of houses in the far back of the amusement park. Now here was someone who'd actually experienced that.

The residents, Liz said, had their own entry point, off to the side. There was no need to ever pass through Storytime Hamlet's main entrance gate and come face-to-face with Enchantra, the huge, grotesque witch with the twisted face and out-of-proportion features who presided over Storytime Hamlet. Things, though, could get somewhat creepy late at night. An after-hours amusement park was fertile ground for partiers, for various shenanigans. One of her neighbors—just a few houses down—was an older guy named Jed, who dealt great quantities of marijuana out of his house. He was mellow enough, but claimed to keep a loaded pistol by his bed. Once Liz was woken up in the middle of the night by a cluster of stoned partiers, lost and scared shitless by Humpty-Dumpty's panicked face as he plummeted off the wall to his destruction.

The clouds had multiplied as the temperature increased slightly, although it wasn't extremely hot. Side by side on their towels, they had moved closer together during the course of their long conversation, which hadn't flagged at all. He hadn't thought there would be all that much, really, to say to this Liz person. Still, though, there was an out-of-kilter undertone that Francis couldn't shake off. He hadn't met her in class or at a party. He hadn't found out what her major was, who she hung out with; he hadn't seen her on University Avenue. That stratified college process, he now realized, had been comforting. And without that stratified college process, he was now forced to rely on his own instincts. And relying on his own instincts, it seemed, was often not the best idea. Relying on his own instincts, for one, had rendered him a former college student. Relying on his own instincts had landed him the job at Tillman's Gulf.

The contingent of old people kept up their steady chatter. Now a family wandered in, a mother and three kids, all of them looking quietly resigned at coming to the lake, as if forced to fulfill some sort of obligation. There were none of the expected trappings: no food or beverages, as far as Francis could tell, no beach toys. The mother and her children spent a listless fifteen minutes staring off at the water and then left shortly thereafter.

He and Liz decided to venture into the lake itself, both strolling cautiously down to the water, taking care to avoid the clumps of pebbles and any hidden pitfalls. The group of old people, having had enough of Oonamee Lake, noisily gathered up their chairs and newspapers, decamping for somewhere else.

The lake water was quite cold. He warmed up gradually, incrementally. The silence, now, was striking. Two girls, who looked to be in their early teens, were energetically roaming through the gazebo; they appeared to be talking animatedly. Aside from that, he and Liz had Oonamee Lake entirely to themselves.

It was very still. They moved closer together. She was, Liz said quietly, growing tired. And then she wrapped an arm around him, right here in the water.

26

Liz lived by herself in a small house in the township. The landlords, Mr. and Mrs. Gargano, were an older Italian couple who had a house next door. The Garganos had an enormous, elaborate garden that took up almost the entire backyard, a jungle of tomatoes, peppers, lettuce. Some of the garden's offerings would, from time to time, be thoughtfully placed on Liz's back porch.

Mrs. Gargano also kept Liz well supplied with anisette cookies, difficult at first to get used to with its harsh, unfamiliar licorice flavor. Mr. Gargano made his own mead, which Francis got to sample once, enjoying the novelty of imbibing a drink he'd assumed was a vanished relic of the Middle Ages.

Liz's tiny domicile was old and sturdy, with thick, industrial walls, solid wood floors, a dense white ceiling. A vase of flowers occupied a prominent spot in her living room, but the house was basically unadorned. There was a framed photo of a beloved, deceased cat; a commemorative graduation mug from Kittahicken High. There were no photos of friends, parents, siblings. In Annie's cramped bed in her compact bedroom, he would awaken to a gallery of photos spread out over the walls: her entire family, including grandparents, nephews, nieces. Liz's bedroom wall was absolutely empty; devoid of a single photo.

There was nothing whatsoever in Liz to remind him of Annie; neither in temperament nor body type. It made a certain amount of sense. If his old life up north was to be abandoned, obliterated, Liz could serve as the physical manifestation.

Francis found her a combination of the idiosyncratic and the commonplace. Exotic, flavored coffees were one of her newfound passions, something he was entirely unfamiliar with. Her deceased cat had, quirkily enough, never actually been given a proper name, referred to during her lifetime as simply "the cat" or "pussycat." There were an array of self-help books scattered around the house: in the living room, bedroom, even the kitchen, as if Liz couldn't function without the recourse of grabbing a book wherever she happened to be. Her divorced parents lived in the general vicinity. She was not in touch with them; not at all, not ever.

Liz had also spent an inordinate amount of time at the rough-hewn bars on Bay Street. She hinted strongly of darker things, an interest in bars and clubs that transcended the casual. There was a massively turbulent past relationship with some lowlife scum who, in her words, deserved to rot in jail for the rest of his life. She had suffered through a host of dead-end jobs during her time in Cherry Hill. She'd been fired from a clothing store in Cape May, had worked as a counselor for at-risk teens in Vineland.

Francis barely, if ever, mentioned anything related to Tillman's; certainly nothing whatsoever in the way of specifics. His job at the gas station was utterly and completely compartmentalized, a strange, sequestered time slot that ceased to exist the moment his puny blue Chevette pulled away from the station and sped along the Expressway. College and the life up north had been the exact opposite: a hodgepodge, an interconnected swirl of people and places and events.

His life now was the opposite of a swirl. He existed in a series of discrete time slots. And that series of discrete time slots came with its own vernacular. "Where have you *been?*" Liz had queried one of the first times she had ever phoned him, and he'd been genuinely nonplussed. Had he forgotten to call her or meet her somewhere? But this query, as he came to quickly comprehend, was simply a bit of quirkiness of Liz's part and didn't necessitate any concrete answer. "Where have you *been?*" was simply her way of initiating a phone conversation.

He had also, somehow, gotten into the habit of greeting Cliff with the identical salutation upon each and every beginning of a shift. *What's the good word?* Francis would call out to him with an element of exaggerated jocularity, to which Cliff would answer back: *Life, man. Life is good.* And then there were times Cliff would turn the tables on him, calling out his own *What's the good word?* to which Francis would be the one to reply: *Life, man. Life is good.*

"Hi, Pops!" Joe would call out to Dutch—each and every time—at the beginning of his shift. And then there was Dutch with the intermittent *Keep your eyes open out there.* And Sonny's *It's fucked-up, kid* and the occasional *It's all your fault, kid.* And it was scary to contemplate just how many times a day Francis said the same things to customers: *May I help you? Thank you. Sign here, please.* Hour after hour, day after day, like a demented parrot, endlessly croaking out the same snatches of conversation: *May I help you? May I help you? Thank you. Thank you. Thank you. May I help you?*

27

One morning Sonny had unexpectedly brought his children—a little boy and girl—into the station. He was surprisingly gentle with them, arms around them both, smiling down at them from atop his great girth, tousling the little boy's hair.

Sonny was, Francis had begun to realize, the watchful force behind Tillman's Gulf, tallying up the shift proceeds, doing the odd repair, unobtrusively observing the Barbarians when they swept into the station. By unspoken arrangement, it seemed, Sonny alone was allowed to flout the Tillman's Gulf dress code, his regulation orange shirt often so unbuttoned that it functioned, in essence, as a simple accoutrement to his white undershirt, which was almost fully exposed.

And he could also be very funny, with a display of irony that was the equivalent of any supposedly clever interchange at the student center or in the commons. Francis had been taking lunch at the battered front desk, too absorbed in his chunk of cheese and cluster of grapes to notice Sonny moving back and forth behind the chair, rummaging about the top of the desk, until finally Sonny lurched forward, his face an exaggerated mask of solicitous concern. "Francis, are you comfortable?" he inquired over-earnestly. "I'm not in your way, am I?"

Sonny was in the grips of crippling insomnia, trying one method after another, all to no avail. Francis had gleaned this from snatches of intermittent conversations between Sonny and Dewey. And this was, he had to admit to himself, surprising: His assumption had been that insomnia was a more elite affliction, that gas-station employees ultimately lacked the internal depth to be plagued by sleepless nights. Sonny and Dewey seemed to have a real bond: the powers behind the Tillman's throne.

Sonny had narrowly escaped serious injury one morning. Francis hadn't thought of working at the gas station as a potentially dangerous occupation, but there were risks and some serious risks, at that. Sonny had lifted the hood of a car with mechanical issues, peering into its bowels. The criminally stupid driver—for god knows what reason—had reached in and opened the radiator cap. Nobody at Tillman's ever simply opened the radiator cap. A car was required to pull off to the side and cool down for a sufficient amount of time. Now Francis could see why this was such an ironclad rule. A burst of what seemed like hot, molten lava shot into the air. Sonny, possessed of split-second instincts Francis hadn't expected, bolted off to the side as the torrent of liquid streamed out and onto the concrete. The potential calamity was sobering. Sonny's face had been right there, in the line of fire.

He and Liz, as it turned out, didn't return to Oonamee Lake, although they certainly intended to. Ultimately, it seemed like too much of an effort. And so the summer proceeded, many of its normal rhythms intact: forays to the beach, the Dairy Queen, pizza and lemonade on the boardwalk. They journeyed to the casinos, eschewing the actual gambling, wandering around strictly as observers, taking in the frenetic slot-machine activity, the boisterousness of craps, and the serious, high-stakes baccarat, which invfolved official observers—akin to tennis judges or lifeguards—perched high above the participants. They drifted into one of the lounges. A coarse standup comedian attempted to entertain the indifferent crowd, the dubious highlight of his repertoire a string of jokes about Stevie Wonder.

As Francis was now an official devotee of Sal's, he took Liz along with him for his first ever in-person visit. And Sal's, one could see immediately, had indeed been an old church, a few sturdy, wooden pews in the back of the restaurant still in existence, where one could presumably take a seat and ponder this odd metamorphosis: from house of worship to cheesesteak dispensary. The fat, bearded malcontent driver who supplied Francis with his cheesesteaks and pizzasteaks was nowhere to be seen.

The mechanics of sub shops always interested him. Even Liz seemed intrigued: The rapid, seemingly chaotic process of sub construction, the sizzling, sputtering grill with onions and cheese at the ready, the stacks and stacks of rolls, sodas and bags of potato chips off to the side.

They had lunch at Will Scarlet's. It was a large restaurant with a very noticeable bright red exterior, located right before one entered the Point. It had never occurred to Francis to actually eat there, as if Will Scarlet's was solely a conspicuous backdrop to indicate the boundary of the Point, its function purely utilitarian. And he felt slightly surprised, as he and Liz entered, to discover a crowded restaurant—so crowded that it necessitated the services of a hostess. Will Scarlet's, all along, had been a real place with real food.

They were well into their lunch when he glanced around. A few tables away was, in the flesh, Admiral Neptune. Francis recognized him instantaneously, immediately alerting Liz. They both looked over and tried not to gape, so thunderstruck at being in the presence of Admiral Neptune.

Admiral Neptune, they could see now, was very elderly. An older woman sat next to him at the table; certainly Mrs. Admiral Neptune, both of them engrossed in their Will Scarlet's lunch. Francis wondered, momentarily, if Larry Veniero would be joining them, but the table was set up for only two. He felt a ripple of unease. What if Admiral Neptune screamed at the waitress or was overheard telling a smutty joke? One's childhood illusions could be ripped apart at a moment's notice, right here during lunch. This, though, didn't seem likely.

A few moments later, a slow realization came over Francis. Admiral Neptune, here at Will Scarlet's, was wearing his distinctive nautical cap, the jaunty headgear he always sported on his show. Anyone with only a cursory knowledge of Admiral Neptune knew about that large, blue cap with its hodgepodge of zany iconography: an anchor, a fish, a tugboat. Apparently, Admiral Neptune never broke character. Even in his off-hours—like eating lunch at Will Scarlet's—he remained Admiral Neptune. There was something both fascinating and disconcerting about seeing this.

28

A creaky-looking, multi-colored Pinto appeared in his lane, disgorging two grimy-looking guys who requested five dollars' worth of gas and then inconsiderately wandered off to the Garden House. This was a perpetual annoyance— drivers who left their cars in the lane and went off for one reason or another, somehow unaware that other cars could possibly materialize and impede everyone's progress. If a driver disappeared for too long and the lane happened to get very crowded, the incoming cars needed to be shunted off to the adjoining lane, a chaotic process that completely disrupted Tillman's normal traffic pattern. And sure enough, as these two occupants returned, laden down with bags of chips and large sodas, some cars had now pulled up.

The Pinto moved on. A split-second later Francis spotted a white baggie on the ground, positioned roughly where the Pinto's back tire had been. He reached down and in one, fluid motion scooped up this white baggie and stuffed it into his pocket. Nobody, as far as he could tell, had observed this. The Pinto's occupants, if they realized what had happened, would certainly be disinclined to return to Tillman's Gulf and inquire as to the whereabouts of a baggie filled with white powder.

A few minutes later, he examined it with fascination in the bathroom stall. It had to be coke. He had always been too apprehensive to ever actually try cocaine, but he'd certainly seen it often enough. Now, emboldened by this pilferage, he felt ready to make the leap.

That evening he shared his discovery with Liz, who seemed pleasantly surprised at this offering. They sat in her kitchen, the shades drawn, as she busied herself in preparation with an expertise and assurance that Francis couldn't help but notice.

He tried to tamp down some growing unease. The coke had been, of course, his idea, but the undercurrent of fear had begun to gnaw at him. He tried not to reflect on the elevator incident, but it was impossible not to; it was one of those horrible incidents he always returned to. This had happened when he was exploring the notion of signing up for work-study: another desperate attempt at salvaging what was left of his scholastic career.

The work-study office was in a building on the far end of campus on the third floor. He had boarded the elevator with two other guys. The elevator bumped along on its slow ascent to the third floor. And then it came to a jolting stop.

The expected resumption of service never transpired. They were stuck. The sudden, overwhelming realization was startling. Even more startling was the sheer weight of his ensuing panic. The panic was notable in and of itself, taking on the properties of a physical manifestation: a giant wave of fear crashing into him. The elevator walls, it felt like, were closing in. He was trapped, utterly and overwhelmingly trapped, confined to this coffin-like elevator, suspended here in nothingness. There was no possible means of escape from the galloping, freakish torrents of fear. "Oh my god," he heard a tiny, faraway voice say. And that tiny, faraway voice was his. And then that tiny, faraway voice said it again: "Oh my god." And the panic, amazingly, only increased, growing exponentially. And then, somehow, the person with that tiny, faraway voice found himself sitting on the elevator floor.

"Hey," one of the guys exclaimed now, a bright, cheery sort who—from Francis's vantage point of sitting on the elevator floor—appeared to be very tall. "Are you signing up for work-study too?" He was smiling broadly and the enthusiasm in his voice was unmistakable. Both of these two guys, in fact, were smiling very, very broadly. "I finished all that awful paperwork," this person continued heartily, waving a collection of papers in a display of good-natured exasperation. And then the second occupant— equally cheerful—joined in. As far as they both knew, they told Francis now, gazing down at him as he huddled in the corner, work-study only involved jobs in the library: the circulation desk, shelving the books. Was the library, though, the only work-study opportunity? Did anyone, per chance, know if there were other options?

It quickly hit Francis that he was being handled. These two well-meaning students were coping as best they could with a hysteric's behavior. And it was him: He was the hysteric. Through his panicked haze he didn't know whether to be grateful or mortified; he settled on a combination of both. The chattering continued: good-natured griping about all the red tape, the typical college bureaucracy. The elevator again resumed its slow ascent.

When the doors opened to the third floor, Francis exited immediately, steadfastly avoiding the gaze of his two companions. There was no thought at all of mustering any remaining dignity. He slunk through the hallway, blindly searching for an exit, and then bolted down the stairway as quickly as he could. When he reached the outside, he felt numb, completely shaken, burning with bewildered shame. And that was it for work-study.

Liz had divided up the coke into little lines, expertly rolling up a ten-dollar bill for snorting purposes. She went first. He managed to push his trepidation aside and followed her lead. Cocaine, he knew, was supposed to rev one up, but very quickly a floating, almost hallucinatory spell came over him.

They had moved to her bed. The house hummed with a sort of quiet. For a time, they could hear Mr. and Mrs. Gargano outside, the clang of gardening implements, cheery conversation. Within an hour's time the Garganos had completed their tasks and all was silent outside the house as well. He and Liz sank onto the bed. Strange, pleasurable waves took hold of him, floating in and out.

29.

For the next few weeks the graveyard shift became his steady beat. It didn't take much, really, to adapt to this odd mode of existence that was in direct opposite to the rest of the world's schedule: working all night, sleeping during the day, going back to work.

The station would still be operating almost full-tilt when he'd arrive a few minutes before eleven; a mass of cars. He would have just enough time to run over to the Garden House for a Coke or Dr Pepper, maybe something for Dewey or Cliff. That Haverford student he'd been so taken with, Francis realized, was gone, perhaps scared off by abrasive customers, disreputable bikers, authoritarian state troopers. And then that may not have been it at all, not even close, he reflected in one of his rueful moments, of which there were many. Perhaps she had left to take summer classes, busy with an intensive regimen of French literature or Chaucer, back to her real life, which without a doubt was a rarefied, studious milieu. Her stint at the Garden House would be viewed as a short-lived mistake, some temporary aberration.

The graveyard shift's first hour or so was the most intensely grueling, with him, Dewey, and Cliff rarely pausing for even a moment.

Francis saw another California plate, a New Mexico. A jazz bassist, performing in some sort of festival in Philly, pulled in driving a surprisingly beat-up car, his bass protruding from the backseat. One older customer actually had no voice, communicating via a device that seemed attached to his throat, his utterances akin to the metallic, robotic tones of old science fiction movies. The transaction ended with an inflectionless, mechanical *thank you*. Some of the drivers, completely heedless of their surroundings, would plow straight ahead and smash into the curb. This, luckily, did not occur with the same regularity as the drivers who would run over the bright orange traffic cones that were placed on either end of a closed lane. That sort of thing happened at semi-regular intervals. It got to the point where Francis knew this had happened without even seeing it, becoming attuned to the distinctive *whomp* of a car barreling over a traffic cone. And those traffic cones, in general, caused no end of confusion. An orange traffic cone perched at either end of a lane seemed unambiguous enough: It meant that the lane, obviously, was inoperative. But customers inquired on a steady basis if these orange cones meant the lane was, in fact, closed. Deductive powers of reasoning evaporated at Tillman's Gulf.

A noisy carload of heavily made-up, abrasively exuberant girls, obviously en route to a night of heady fun, took a liking to Cliff, all of them chorusing out *party hardy* to him as they drove off, although the invocation to party hardy couldn't have fallen on deafer ears than Cliff's.

The graveyard shift was when the scattered limos would arrive. Limos were often a nighttime phenomenon, less of a commodity during the day. Those anonymous, massive vehicles were slightly intimidating, although the uniformed drivers, as a rule, were certainly pleasant enough. Francis never knew if these limos were occupied or not. They were most probably the domain of the casinos, utilized to transport high-rollers. A wide array of perks, apparently, were available to these high-rollers. Sometimes he wondered if sex was involved and concluded that yes, it probably was. He thought back to the older man at the lounge bar, the younger woman he had departed with.

The opening stretch of the graveyard shift was a dark, hot progression of steady labor. Within the hour Francis's hair would be matted down with sweat, his face smudged. As time progressed, his body and hair began collecting additional layers of sweat, which would dry and then collect anew. At least he could momentarily run off to the side, take some swigs of soda, and then resume his duties.

123

In the middle of all the frenetic activity there would be the inevitable appearance of a large, luxurious automobile, gliding smoothly, serenely, almost noiselessly, to the pump. The driver would be a middle-aged, tanned husband, along with his middle-aged, tanned wife. The woman would be wearing a brightly colored, fancy dress; the man's attire would be formal but casual at the same time: a pastel jacket, crisp slacks. These sort of customers could be expected to make an appearance at least once a night, adhering to some sort of unofficial requirement that luxurious cars with well-groomed, tanned middle-aged couples needed to pull into the station on a steady basis.

The car door might swing open for just a few moments, accompanied by that soothing *ding-ding-ding*, almost like chimes. Francis would be hit by a sudden blast of the car's cool, treated air—a godsend, this little burst of air-conditioning on an intensely hot, sweaty night. The car would smell new, clean; permeated with a faint but discernible mixture of cologne and perfume, its radio tuned to the soothing beautiful-music station: Mantovani and cascading strings, the sounds of waves in the background during the station breaks. When Francis was much younger he had assumed that this was a physical actuality, that the announcer was, in fact, speaking in close proximity to the ocean.

The man and woman, of course, would have not a drop of sweat or discomfort on them, protected as they were from the nighttime heat. And they would be unfailingly courteous—smiling, even—toward the smudged gas-station attendant.

And then the car would glide away as noiselessly as it had arrived. For the briefest of brief moments Francis would actually be startled to find himself here at Tillman's Gulf, sweaty and hot, wearing a bright-orange Gulf shirt and blue work pants, staring down at a long, endless line of cars.

***

The consensus, during these late-night hours, was that the crazies would begin to emerge. It was a steady refrain he'd hear from customers on the graveyard shift and from some of the state troopers: *The crazies are out tonight* or *It must be a full moon* or *Where'd these people get their licenses?*

The late hours created an odd sort of intimacy on the part of some customers. Many of the drivers felt a friendly obligation to provide a running update on what was transpiring around the station: The traffic coming out of Philly was especially backed up, or there'd been some kind of accident on the Parkway. From time to time a well-meaning customer would offer a bottle of beer—something, of course, Francis always had to refuse. Accepting alcohol was absolutely verboten at Tillman's Gulf, a surefire way of getting fired.

A waitress pulled in, recounting a frantic tale. She was running late for her shift and in a manner both commanding and imploring, thrust a five-dollar bill into Francis's hand along with a hastily scrawled note: the phone number, she explained, for Warren the manager. Could he call and let Warren know Luanne was on her way? And so, with a nod of assent from Dewey, Francis ran into the station and made the call. This Warren person was unfazed—thankful, even—to be receiving this phone call, finding it in the realm of the quotidian to be chatting with an anonymous employee of Tillman's Gulf and learning that Luanne was on her way.

Around one o'clock, the volume of customers began to decrease just enough to make things more bearable, less fever-pitched. Francis could catch his breath, gulp down some more Dr Pepper. When Dewey had begun working at Tillman's Gulf all those years ago, he'd related to Francis and Cliff, the nighttime was almost entirely deserted. The Expressway was so sparsely traveled that he and he alone had worked the graveyard shift. The Garden House didn't exist then. He could even go out for a little walk, wander around at three in the morning, smoke a cigarette, and if a car did happen to pull into the station he could hear it and make his way back. That's how quiet it was. Around ten miles away was a poorly managed Sinclair station that attracted almost no customers. It had finally gone out of business, leaving the field entirely to Tillman's Gulf. The Sinclair dinosaur, which had towered over the station for years, remained standing long after the actual station had ceased to exist.

30

Val had been employed at the Garden House since it first opened. In fact, for years and years she and Dewey had often worked their respective graveyard shifts in tandem. If Tillman's grew progressively quieter as the long night stretched on, the situation at the Garden House was even more pronounced. Getting gas was a necessity. But at three in the morning, not many drivers could be induced to voluntarily spend time at the Garden House. Their overpriced cheeseburgers and scalding, industrial-strength coffee could never in a million years be construed as a necessity. It was enough, really, to simply construe the Garden House's food as edible.

Val did her best to ensure that those working the Tillman's graveyard shift didn't have to pay for their Garden House purchases of chips, soda, pretzels. She wasn't able to always accomplish this. Things, at times, could get tricky. The young, know-it-all manager was occasionally still on the premises. This manager, according to Val, was desperate to exert what little piddling authority he had. In reality, he knew next to nothing about the ins and outs of the Garden House and, in fact, had his head so far up his butt that he never saw daylight. Val and the rest of the Garden House staff—as opposed to their idiot boss—knew the workings of the place inside out.

Francis certainly knew this manager on sight, who looked like a state trooper: short, bristling hair and with the obvious eyes of a fanatic, filled with a burning zealousness to run the Garden House with an iron hand. You could see him off to the side, staring at the proceedings, correcting a hapless employee on how to best refill the ketchup or stock the sugar packets. Among his other faults, Val reported back, was a woeful, unforgivable ignorance of the rudiments of customer service: making the customer feel at home, putting travelers at ease, bantering with road-weary children.

There had always been a loose, informal alliance of sorts between Tillman's Gulf and the Garden House. Food and soda would be offered gratis; Tillman's provided some free mechanical help for Val and a few of the others. But Mr. Head-Up-His-Butt Manager—either because of sheer stupidity or blatant disregard—directly contravened this longstanding tradition between the two businesses. He had let it be known in no uncertain terms that favoritism of any sort did not exist at the Garden House. Efficiency and professionalism were now the top priorities. And so, when Francis would come in for sodas and chips for him and Dewey and Cliff, Val would matter-of-factly ring up the sale, take Francis's money, and—in the guise of dispensing change—would simply hand him back the whole amount. All this transpired, of course, without a word or acknowledgment from either of them. And so, right under the nose of Mr. Efficiency and Professionalism, these new, supposedly nonnegotiable rules were being openly flouted.

The manager rarely, if ever, stayed past one o'clock in the morning. As soon as he exited the premises, the entire Garden House breathed a collective sigh of relief.

In all likelihood this moron wouldn't last long. Val had survived an endless series of short-lived reigns by delusional, power-hungry half-wits.

The sparse activity at the Garden House gave Val regular opportunities to drop by the station during the dead of night. There was no husband in her life, although Francis had no idea of the circumstances, if she was divorced or widowed. She often mentioned Lindy, her teenaged daughter, with obvious pride. They were more like sisters than mother and daughter, Val would say; inseparable. From what Francis could perceive, she was not exaggerating. Val and Lindy shopped together, went out to dinner in Cape May together, even bowled together on the same team. Val promised to bring in a group photo, which she did. It made Francis sad. She was so utterly unaware of bowling's blue-collar connotations. Perusing the photo made him even sadder: A whole array of women in their team shirts, all of them smiling delightedly at the camera, blissfully ignorant of their consigned socio-economic role. Lindy could be identified immediately, a younger, prettier version of Val, but with much shorter hair.

Francis knew Dewey had a teenaged daughter, who he barely mentioned. His ex-wife, though, was the occasional target of his sarcastic barbs. This ex-wife, Dewey had related to him and Val in the course of some of their late-night talks, had recently reverted back to her maiden name. Dewey was, in his own words, tickled pink to hear this. *Tickled pink*, in fact, seemed to be the only plausible reaction to learning that one's ex-wife had gone back to her maiden name, because Dewey repeated the phrase on several occasions during the week. "I was tickled pink," he insisted—many times—to Val and to Sonny as well. Francis found himself genuinely surprised. He hadn't imagined that Dewey's ex-wife—whoever she was—would have the assertiveness and knowledge to switch back to her maiden name. His assumption was that nobody in her milieu ever exercised that option.

Dewey's mother was old and infirm. He seemed exceedingly devoted to her. Francis couldn't help but notice his warmth and thoughtfulness when older customers came into the station, the acerbic exterior melting away, taking it upon himself to wash their windows—something, as a rule, he never did—ending the transactions with an even more uncharacteristic "God bless you."

Some nights Val brought in her homemade chocolate-chip or sugar cookies. She had mentioned more than once that it was lasagna, not cookies, that was her real specialty. She was famed for her lasagna, as Lindy could attest. And then Val, in an amazingly expansive gesture, actually brought some of it in for Francis and Dewey, arriving at the gas station at three in the morning with a pan of her aromatic lasagna, freshly heated up via the Garden House's oven, so hot that the cheese was still bubbling away.

And what an odd trio they made—Francis and Dewey and Val sitting in the Tillman's office, digging into the thick slabs of steaming lasagna. There was something slightly dreamlike in all of this.

There was something dreamlike, actually, in all of it. For one, working the graveyard shift engendered a lot of fatigue, combined with a total disruption of his normal rhythms. He'd awaken at three in the afternoon, for example, sometimes instinctively craving breakfast.

There was more, though, than just fatigue and disorientation. The long work stretch instantly evaporated from his mind as soon as the graveyard shift came to an end. He forgot about Tillman's Gulf at approximately 7:15 and didn't think of it again until that night at approximately 10:45, when he entered the far left lane of the Expressway and exited into the gas station. There was a whiff of the unreal in his dealings with Dewey and Val: a reoccurring, elaborate dream.

31

At two o'clock in the morning, Cliff would finish up his shift. To Francis, this was the oddest shift, time-wise: six at night until two in the morning. On occasion, he'd been stuck with working the six-to-two. Six-to-two was neither fish nor fowl. It was the outlier shift.

The cars, by two o'clock, had greatly reduced in number. This was when activity truly quieted down. By three o'clock some carloads of sleeping people would show up, the driver speaking very quietly or even whispering, loathe to wake up his passengers—which sometimes involved conked-out children—mouthing a *thank-you* to Francis or flashing a thumbs-up sign.

An old, beat-up car pulled in around three in the morning. In and of itself, this was not unusual, but the occupants were a mother and her little boy. What was a kid doing up so late? "Give the man the money," the mother urged, and the boy shyly handed over a ten-dollar bill, to which Francis offered his thanks, and then—with the solemnity befitting such a transaction—officially passed back the requisite change not to the mother, but to the child. And the little boy, emboldened, asked Francis if he was going to have dessert now. And this too made Francis horribly, horribly sad, although it was difficult to articulate why this was so.

Large trucks would loudly, forcibly come into the station, many of them bearing faraway license plates, the drivers often taking advantage of the dearth of customers to amble over to the Garden House for some sustenance. Some were of the rough-hewn variety and not very friendly. "A bunch of niggers ripped me off in Camden," one of the drivers shouted, almost exuberantly, as he drove in, the racial epithet sailing out over the gas pumps and the empty lanes.

The night crawled: The jovial airport-shuttle guy with the wild swirl of a toupee. A car from Alabama. A limo. More trucks. A middle-aged customer got out of his car to stretch his limbs and promptly farted. A flat-out drunk drove in; this time Dewey was the one to sic the state troopers on him.

The bright station lights accentuated the dark night that surrounded them. Tillman's Gulf seemed a small oasis in the huge, black expanse of the Expressway. A dirty, well-lighted place. Three o'clock was when Francis felt the beginning prickles of fatigue, of sleepiness.

In the corner of the office was a bare-bones, utilitarian black-and-white TV set. Scarcely noticeable—and off-limits—during the busy daytime, it could be utilized in the dead of night. Because of the late hour and perhaps because of their locale, the television picked up bits and pieces that didn't exist in the daytime. For three nights a Baltimore station, of all things, came briefly into focus, then vanished, never to appear again. One night, around four in the morning, there was a faint, barely viewable broadcast from Connecticut—also never to reappear. At this hour there wasn't much to watch: some old movies, the news. *Gunsmoke* was aired at three-thirty on channel 41. And then sermonettes, the national anthem, test patterns, snow.

At around four-thirty, five, you'd see the occasional fishermen, all awake and energetic, their day just beginning. An energetic, ruddy fisherman opened his truck door for whatever reason. He had opened it, though, too energetically, and it swung back on its own accord, knocking off his fisherman's hat while Francis bit his lip to keep from laughing.

Farm trucks also began to show up, chugging in with their full loads of tomatoes, blueberries, peaches. One farmer took pity on him, this hot and weary gas-station attendant, thoughtfully offering Francis two peaches, which he gratefully wolfed down. In the back of his mind there was the dim awareness that he harbored a slight peach sensitivity. Now he discovered that quickly consuming two ripe peaches, one after the other, led to his left cheek swelling to double its size. It was an odd physical state that lasted a good hour, as if he had crammed in a wad of chewing tobacco.

And then began the slow, almost imperceptible transition. The dead of night—that absolute dead of night—began to shift, inflected by the first, faint strains of the approaching morning. The darkness was no longer absolutely pitch-black, the contours of the night beginning, now, to subtly alter. Darkness began to grow softer. The air itself underwent its own subtle gradations, smelling just a little sweeter. The gas pumps, the shed, began to come into focus, the silver tops of the pumps beginning to glisten—just a bit—with sunlight. The small trucks and scattered cars that came into Tillman's now seemed more visible, three-dimensional. License plates could be read with greater ease, the bright station lights no longer absolutely necessary to decipher the letters and numbers.

Had he really been at this all night long? Along with his increasing fatigue, there were the first pinpricks of hunger.

And then Francis's gaze would travel beyond the shed, beyond the gas pumps, beyond the Philly-bound lanes, beyond the entire station. His eyes took in the quiet Expressway and even, as best as his vision would allow, beyond that as well. The pine trees that lined the highway were starting to take form, emerging in the slow daylight, the green filling in. Behind the pine trees were, of course, more pine trees, the woods. He could hear the chirping of birds. A mist began to rise slowly over the trees; blankets of mist, everything quiet and soft, the only audible sounds the exuberant calls and chirps of the birds.

The smell of bacon and cooking food wafted over from the Garden House. In those moments, Tillman's Gulf ceased to exist. It was a cool summer morning in the country, before the heat of the day. There was no gas station, no Expressway, no Garden House, no cars. The mist rose over the pines on this country morning. The birds called to each other.

32

The traffic, as seven o'clock approached, began to pick up. Now Francis was truly exhausted, awaiting the arrival of the day shift. He actually felt a little sorry for them, the idea of having to begin a whole, entire shift.

Sonny, as always, was the first to arrive, parking his pickup off to the side, his shirt already unbuttoned almost all the way down. "Hi, kid," he would say, nodding, and Francis would stand rigidly at attention, something that never failed to amuse Sonny, who would head straight to the office to confer with Dewey, discussing the night's take, if there'd been any repairs or special concerns, if Mr. Tillman was planning on coming in today. And then Dutch arrived, already smoking a cigarette. Lord Haw-Haw was next, always irritatingly early. Joe would drive in right before seven, perhaps after the completion of his other eight-hour stint, calling out "Hi, Pops" to Dutch, his usual salutation.

But Francis's shift was over. He was done. Sonny would already be ensconced at the desk in the creaky chair, cigarette dangling from his mouth, stirring his Dunkin' Donuts coffee with the end of his pencil. Francis would hand over his roll of money. "It's all your fault, kid," Sonny would tell him, and then Dutch would assume his sentry-like perch near the shed, two packs of cigarettes at the ready. Francis would wobble his way to the bathroom for the satisfying, post-shift piss and then proceed to the garage to utilize the scalding powdered soap over the old sink, washing the grime off his hands and arms, catching a glimpse in the dirty, cracked mirror of the tired and smudged face. And Francis was always surprised to see that tired, smudged face, which looked as if it had been pumping gas all night.

By the time he completed his ablutions, the day shift was up and running, the number of cars already substantial. He felt an overwhelming sense of relief as he plopped himself into the Chevette for the ride home. The first few times he'd driven home after working all night long he'd come perilously close to falling asleep at the wheel. He'd assumed this had to be a physical impossibility, that the level of engagement driving demanded would easily override any sleep reflex from kicking in. This wasn't true: One could really and truly fall asleep while driving. It was near impossible, utterly unaccustomed as he was to graveyard shifts, to keep his eyes open. He was forced to roll his window all the way down, which provided only momentary alertness. In desperation, he rolled the passenger-seat window down, and then the rest of the windows as well. Francis's sleepiness increased. He turned on the radio, made it louder, and finally increased the volume to ear-splitting levels. And this is how he proceeded down the Expressway: all windows wide open, WMMR cranking out at top volume.

Luckily, he'd grown much more acclimated to staying alert on the drive home, although it did require mustering up his last reserves of strength, listening to the radio—loud, but not at all on full volume—and using the allure of Buzby's coconut pancakes as a reward.

Arriving at Buzby's, he would feel a slight pride at his dishevelment. The uniform, smudges, and weariness signified rough-and-tumbleness, someone certainly deserving of coconut pancakes and coffee after an honest night's toil. Buzby's, at this early hour, was almost deserted. He soon became a recognized customer to the staff, ushered into his very own booth.

And then, infused with pancakes and coffee, he began the final leg of his journey, driving homeward while the rest of the country was just beginning their day. The roads, this early in the morning, were often entirely deserted; for miles and miles his would be the only car in evidence. On Patcong Drive were the remnants of an old, crumbling grocery store and its weather-beaten sign with *Fresh Corn* in large, faded letters. Once, while zipping down

Patcong, he was startled to see—smack in the very middle of the road—a looming black garbage bag, like some sort of booby trap. Instantly alert now, he swerved to avoid it, then glanced at his rearview mirror. The large black garbage bag had vanished. What the hell was this? Then there was a sudden jolt to the car, as if he'd run over a squirrel, and when he again glanced at the rearview mirror he could see dollops of garbage spilling out of his car in a straight, symmetrical trail. What he'd done, of course, was inadvertently run over this garbage bag, which had attached itself to the underside of the Chevette. As if he'd been undertaking an impeccably crafted, malevolent prank, the bag had systematically emptied itself of its garbage, yielding a straight line of trash running all down Patcong Drive. And then, finally, the shredded garbage bag itself was disgorged. This was the crowning *fuck you* to this inadvertent act of road vandalism. If there were any doubts as to the source of this garbage, here were the remains—in plain sight—of the offending black garbage bag.

When Francis arrived home, the family would be in the throes of their preparation for the normal workday. He took a hot, rejuvenating shower and fell into a deep, air-conditioned slumber. Arising, he would peruse that morning's *Journal-Bulletin*, taking comfort in *Miss Peach* and *Tumbleweeds*, the advice columns. He would order a sub from Sal's, and—if the mood struck—immerse himself in *Pomp and Circumstance*. And that was that.

33.

Mr. Tillman switched Francis back to the day shift. Now he was again in sync, more or less, with the rest of the world, rising along with his parents and Jeanette, all of them heading out to work together. He had grown inured to Jeanette's concept of both of them heading out to their respective stations. There was even an element of fleeting pride. Let others like Jeanette go off to their cushy stations. He was heading out to a *real* station, one that involved wearing a workingman's uniform and performing arduous physical labor. That pride, of course, was sporadic.

He welcomed the return of normal circadian rhythms, but found the day shift surprisingly disorienting. That distinctive subterranean feel to the graveyard shift had vanished without a trace. Norm, Joe's friend, would be working the eleven-to-seven for the time being, and Francis felt an unexpected wistfulness for Val's cookies and lasagna, the strange glimpses of faraway TV stations at three in the morning, and his after-work routine at Buzby's: coconut pancakes, coffee, a booth all to himself.

The day shift was an unexpected strain. He'd forgotten just how hot and crowded this shift could be, how demanding the customers could get. Rude or clueless customers were not, of course, unknown on the graveyard shift. But they were something of a rarity, the drivers probably too fatigued to be properly abrasive. There were no such strictures during the day. "Fill the tank, check the oil, check the transmission," one driver had imperiously snapped out at him, as if Francis was his servant. Then there were the drivers who requested directions and stopped listening the moment he began dispensing the information. This, to his intense irritation, happened often.

He'd almost forgotten about Eddie and Lord Haw-Haw. Eddie had become slightly more sedate, less inclined to spin tales of grit and bravery, to exhort one and all to go to church. He was more apt, these days, to complain about his wife, who nagged him relentlessly and seemed unable to appreciate his true worth.

Lord Haw-Haw had begun a semi-regular mopping regimen, undertaking a sopping-wet cleanup of the office and the back of the station. Francis didn't know if he'd taken this task of his own volition or it had been assigned to him, but Lord Haw-Haw tackled the task with his typical zeal. It was an inept zeal, though—the first time around he had gotten the large pail, filled to the brim with water, somehow wedged into the opened door, and a minute later the pail tipped over and sent a huge volume of water cascading into the office. Francis hadn't seen Sonny move so quickly since that customer had uncorked the radiator. He and Eddie stood by the pumps, watching with a mixture of horror and awe at how much water really did fit into the large pail.

Mr. Tillman was a semi-regular presence, showing up a few times a week, basically sequestered in the office. Although Mr. Tillman never stayed longer than a few hours at a stretch, he would nonetheless take the time and effort to garb himself in a resplendent Gulf uniform—a general in full regalia.

The line of cars stretched on and on and on; an unending procession. Francis began to wish for an overtly intoxicated driver, someone he could rat out to the troopers.

In the midst of an intensely busy shift this one car pulled into his lane. A large blanket was draped over its contents in the back. This car was loaded up, packed full: a stereo, two suitcases, some boxes and bags, scattered albums and cassettes. A big box of Tide detergent, Francis could see, was perched in the backseat, seemingly unanchored to anything at all and ripe for spillage. It wasn't time for the advent of the fall semester, but he didn't have the slightest doubt in the world that this driver, this car—

the suitcases and boxes and bags and albums and large blanket and big box of Tide—was heading to school.

When summers would come to an end and it was time for the resumption of college, Francis would carefully disconnect his stereo, hoping to remember how to reconnect it later. He would gather up his albums, and then attempt to pack his clothes with some sense of rudimentary organization. His mother would remind him to include warmer, heavier items of clothing for later in the semester, which he did, enjoying the cognitive dissonance of packing sweaters and thick corduroys while the summer sun blazed outside. His mother also insisted he take along exactly two towels, bars of soap, toothpaste, and a new toothbrush, as if he was heading out to a rugged place where soap and toothpaste were rare commodities.

The soap was always Irish Spring and nothing but. Interestingly, Irish Spring was never used in their household. On that very first day of freshman year, the college had thoughtfully provided a miniature hygiene kit for incoming students: deodorant, a bar of Irish Spring, and a condom, which had elicited in Francis both a surge of excitement at the possibilities this implied, but which also felt thoroughly intimidating, as if college demanded a high level of sexual proficiency. Irish Spring became his special back-to-college soap, its smell alone generating an instantaneous sensory response that conjured up those first few weeks of a new fall semester, that distinct mélange of hot weather entwined with classes, new books, the commons.

With an almost ceremonial formality, his father would arrange the car and the trunk so that all of Francis's possessions would fit together with near-symmetrical precision. And the drive north commenced with Francis at the wheel, his father riding shotgun, his mother wedged into the backseat.

Within a few short hours he could hear the first, faint strains of those radio stations that he'd listen to fanatically during the semester and missed during his summers home. Periodically, he would spot those other cars on the highway that were loaded up in essentially the same manner, transporting their own back-to-school cargo. Francis could identify them instantaneously, akin to deciphering a code.

He and his parents would arrive in town, pleasantly fatigued, unload the contents of the car, and then they'd all go out to dinner at Gina's, the big jars of parmesan solidly planted on every table, a pizza, salad, and cold pitcher of soda their standard fare.

And so Francis, staring at this car in his lane, was flooded with all those memories, the sensory re-creation so overwhelming that he was too afraid to ask the driver if he was, indeed, going off to school. But he knew the answer without having to ask. Of course this driver was returning to college. A distinct feeling of unease grew in the pit of Francis's stomach and he did his best to avoid direct eye contact with this customer, grateful that in this particular transaction he was not called upon to make change, happy—elated, even—to wait on the next car in line.

That happiness, though, immediately turned to pure hatred at the sight of the next customer, a dour older man who looked as if he'd never seen an actual college in his life. This time Francis's luck didn't hold. He was required to check this stupid piece of shit's oil and make change.

And then, the next week, something even more startling transpired. He was just about to take his lunch of a sandwich, bag of grapes, chunk of Wisconsin cheese wrapped in tinfoil, and oatmeal cookies, when an extremely attractive girl drove into his lane. She seemed immediately familiar, which was, of course, utterly improbable and most likely a bout of wishful thinking. As Francis filled her car, though, he kept glancing at her. The idea that he really and

141

truly did know her from somewhere would not go away; it transcended wishful thinking. He cautiously asked her a few questions and then realized, to his great shock, who she was.

This was the girl who worked at the student center—a funny, friendly presence and dispenser of sodas and chips, almost always on duty when Francis would show up right before afternoon classes. He had bantered with her about *Guiding Light.* They had also discussed the onerousness of arising early in the morning to study, a well-intentioned concept that never, ever panned out.

The sheer improbability of this girl appearing now, right in his lane, seemed providential, and he directed an excited verbal burst through her open car window, a torrent of explanation that encompassed the student center, their *Guiding Light* discussions, the shared aversion to studying so early in the morning. Even as Francis was saying these words to her, he was gripped with the awareness that all this sounded not just inane, but desperate—desperate to the point of looking unhinged. He saw himself through this girl's eyes: One of her college peers, now reduced to pumping gas, babbling about the high point of his life— some long-ago, peripheral encounters at the student center.

And, yes, she did recognize him, reasonably pleased to stumble upon this unexpected coincidence. As she paid for her gas he became hyper-aware of his greasy dishevelment, the callus on his right hand. She offered a friendly, hurried good-bye and, without further ado, departed from the gas station. At most, she would find this an amusing coincidence—if that. Her life, obviously, had progressed. His life, just as obviously, had not.

If Francis had been that sort of decisive, take-charge person, he would have quit his job at Tillman's Gulf right then and there, absolutely unable to bear the indignity of working here for another moment. This would have been the very dramatic turning point in his life: the epiphany. He'd always yearned for a dramatic turning point, an epiphany. He was not, of course, that decisive, take-charge person. His life was devoid of turning points and epiphanies. There was even a lack of *tragic* turning points. The dissolution of things with Annie, the unraveling of his college career—there were a hundred different contributing factors, all adding up to an undefined muddle.

34

What did happen, though, was that the college began to take on almost holy aura: The beauty of University Avenue. Reading Joseph Conrad on the ratty old couch in the apartment. Coffee at the Lebanese restaurant. The ecstasy of the Feedbag's strombolis and frittatas.

He, Philip, and Caleb had discovered this unbelievably cheap Chinese restaurant down by the train station, the interior fashioned entirely in red—the walls, the carpet, the tables—like some sort of forgotten bordello. Lunch, as he recalled, was four dollars apiece. It was a wonder they had all escaped without food poisoning.

He began to reflect on these things more and more. The memories of Somerset Apartments filled him with such tenderness that he came close to choking up. He was nearly moved to tears by the thought of the Brew 'n Wich, the déclassé bar and eatery down the block, a massive stag's head perched above the front door.

The shifts at Tillman's now seemed of unendurable length. He instinctively registered the appearance of a Georgia license plate and then berated himself for even noticing. Who cared? Who gave a fuck about keeping track of license plates? The customers and long lines began to feel intolerable, his heart sinking whenever he was requested to check the oil. Eddie had decided that the 3 Musketeers wrapper—bearing the figures of three colorfully outfitted fops—was gay. It was a joke he began making at regular intervals. Francis could barely look at him. Eddie and the 3 Musketeers joke seemed indicative of his own sorry lot, expelled from the Eden of college life and relegated to listening to half-wits and their inane jokes. He was unable to summon the will to converse at all—even a little bit—with Lord Haw-Haw. From time to time he found himself wishing Dutch would slip and fall off one of the islands.

And then the epiphany he had so longed for did, in fact, transpire, although his particular epiphany moved along at a slower pace than the more dramatic, instantaneous sort of epiphany. His slow-moving epiphany was that the Lebanese restaurant, the Feedbag, University Avenue—all of it, in fact—still existed. This was probably glaringly obvious to the rest of the word, but in his excessive devotion to the memories of this never-never land, Francis had not really considered that one could return there. The knowledge that it was a real place shocked him to the core. One could, theoretically, reenter.

Francis mulled this over for a while. An epiphany required bold, new ways of thinking. He conceived of an ingenious plan, actually calling the *Dispatch*, the newspaper up north, and with a modicum of friendly negotiating, arranged for a month's worth of Sunday editions to be mailed to the house.

He'd been thoroughly discreet about these new plans he was attempting to formulate. His parents and Jeanette perked up with the first arrival of the *Dispatch* in the mail. This was tangible, physical evidence that perhaps there was some substance in what Francis was contemplating. The arrival of the Sunday *Dispatch* in the mail was tangible, physical evidence even to him.

It was startling to see the *Dispatch* here, so weirdly out of context on the kitchen table. *Boner's Ark* was still prominent in their comics constellation. The restaurant review still occupied its slot on the first page of the second section. He and Phillip had always found these reviews especially humorous, explorations of sandwich shops and souvlaki joints, written with an affected, wildly out-of-kilter gravitas.

Everything, he felt slightly chagrined to discover, had continued on without him. The little tailor shop on the corner of Finch and Witherspoon, which had stood in the very same spot for over fifty years, had finally shut its doors. A new ice-cream parlor had opened up next to the religious bookstore.

***

Art had found himself a girlfriend: Trina, one of his coworkers. She was, at first glance, basically humorless, possessed of a single-minded devotion to her career at the Dover. She hailed from Florida and appeared to have moved up here with the express purpose of working at the Dover—an important first step, as she explained more than once, for her career in hotel management. Francis found her unbearably pompous, but on further encounters she had loosened up some, exhibiting a sense of humor. And so, he and Liz and Art and Trina would occasionally while away some evenings at a random bar or restaurant, all of them once hanging out at the Sunspot where—to Francis's relief—the Jetsons weren't in attendance for the night.

Trina, belying those first impressions of stuffiness, actually did a fair amount of drinking on these nights out. It took Francis more time to notice that Liz, at regular intervals, also got fairly inebriated on these outings, but it was the opposite of the loquacious, let-it-all-hang-out school of drunkenness. Liz got quieter, eyes glazed and then half-shut, as if she were stoned, not drunk. He had come no further in cracking the exterior of her tangled family life, with Liz still unwilling to divulge much of anything.

Now that the *Dispatch* was arriving in his mailbox every week, Francis began to affect a mien of bored condescension whenever Art and Trina launched into their passionate discussions of hotel arcana. It all seemed so pedestrian, so provincial. Liz too began to appear hickish in his eyes, her concerns inconsequential. Her secretive family history seemed less an enticing mystery and more a gratuitous hang-up.

He himself was leaving, off to better things. Although, of course, in actuality he hadn't gone anywhere. Nor was he in any way certain what, exactly, those better things were.

***

There certainly was no shortage of available rentals in these empty, quiet days of summer; a slew of people running classifieds in the *Dispatch* who were eager to rent for two months, three months, six. To Francis, the imperative was simply to relocate, to get there. What he would actually do seemed secondary. There were, he could see, all sorts of jobs to be had. Not desirable jobs, certainly, but jobs nonetheless. He could work as an office temp; in a restaurant, a store. And might he return to school? The question hung in the air, unspoken.

Without ceremony, he found a three-month share with two other students in an apartment on Peach Street. He had a general idea of the locale. Peach Street, as he vaguely remembered, was a nondescript, typical little thoroughfare, sturdy small houses and well-tended lawns running up and down the block.

The lack of concrete specifics did give him some pause. This new, upcoming chapter in his life was still undefined. Perhaps this was a disastrous miscalculation; sleepwalking into some sort of personal catastrophe. That, though, didn't seem plausible. Not now. He had actually formulated a plan of action: the apartment, potential employment. There was enthusiasm on the part of his parents and Jeanette. He hoped—fervently—that it was all for the good.

And there were really no other options for him. There was no other place to go.

35

Liz simply melted away—her blond tresses, her cottage, her tangled family history—as if she were a favorite character in a TV show that had completed its run. There was a desultory evening at a bar in the township, Liz mournful and somewhat inebriated. If she was an alcoholic, she told him, now would be the time when she would begin to drink heavily. If she was a binge eater, this is when she would stock up on cookies and junk food. He was inflicting, Francis realized now, a huge measure of pain on her. That wasn't supposed to have happened.

He gave Mr. Tillman the requisite two weeks' notice, who expressed a surprising amount of warmth in learning of Francis's plans. Years before, Mr. Tillman related, one of the summer help had gone on and become a doctor. There was the connotation that Francis was serving as the gas station's emissary, off into the wider world.

They all wished him luck, Joe and Norm and Eddie and even Lord Haw-Haw, Dewey loudly announcing that Francis had been great to work with, had never put on airs, had never acted like he was better than the rest of them. This filled him with a secret pride that seemed way too corny to even admit to himself. And Dewey's statement was a little startling as well, although it shouldn't have been. So it had been noticed all along that he came from a different world, a world of dorms, exams, classrooms.

Dutch shook his hand with a firm grip, told him to keep his eyes open. And then Sonny, apropos of nothing, told him not to fuck up. "I fucked up, kid," he continued, "and ended up here." There was something chilling in this. Sonny had envisioned something other for himself, something greater than this.

"I'll pray for you, man," Cliff told him, and to Francis this seemed almost profound in its heartfelt authenticity, its lack of affect. And then, almost about to enter his car, Val approached, laden with homemade cookies for him and his family. And this too seemed laced with a profundity he couldn't quite articulate.

Art and Trina both thought his plan of action was a superlative one, and again he felt inwardly embarrassed at how flattering, how reassuring this was. They promised to visit, Trina—of course—claiming to know some of the local hotels.

Right before his departure he received a letter from Liz. The language seemed a mixture of the slightly maudlin, with overtones of the phraseology of recovery. She was feeling great, the letter mentioned several times, and she was feeling strong and happy, utilizing a positive attitude that would serve as a fortification for any potential obstacles that would come her way. She had liked him a lot, the letter went on to say. And if she wasn't careful, she might have fallen in love with him. Maybe they would see each other again when there was less going on in their lives. Take care, the letter concluded.

Reading those words was like a burning shock. He had no idea; no clue at all as to Liz's feelings. If he'd been aware of these feelings, though, would it have ultimately mattered? He was leaving. It was too late to ponder any implications. *Take care.*

PART 3

36

The sturdy blue Chevette was packed in the most utilitarian manner as possible. There was not, of course, the high drama of returning to another school year. This had a direct, physical manifestation as well: Many of those typical accoutrements of his college life—like his stereo—were absent from the car. He had emphatically refused to purchase any Irish Spring. Irish Spring was strictly for the beginning of the semester. What he was embarking on now was certainly a resumption; but it was not the resumption of a new semester. It was something nebulous, tinged with hope and uncertainty. Irish Spring would have been inappropriate. Maybe later there would be cause for renewed purchase of it, but not now. Accordingly, he had brought along a package of the almost scentless, neutral Dove soap. His new life now—whatever form it was going to take—required a new soap.

And so he set out. The flat terrain of home began to gradually, incrementally shift. The ocean, always in the background, felt as if it was receding, finally fading out altogether as the geographic focal point. Hills slowly began to make their appearance. The summer sky and its distinctive, vibrant blue turned, in bits and pieces, grittier, less pastoral. Traffic began to thicken. The busy two lanes increased to three.

The puny Chevette cranked along, holding its own. As Francis traveled onward, portions of the mammoth racetrack off to the left could be glimpsed, towering over the landscape. At night it was spectacular, the powerful, colorful lights illuminating the entire structure.

Now, finally, a sense of high drama began to overtake him. The promised land, he thought; he was returning to the promised land, and then had to laugh at his own grandiosity. That phrase, though, kept returning: *The promised land.*

Without ceremony, Francis moved his few possessions into the apartment on Peach Street. His room was tiny and unbearably hot, necessitating a trip to Discountland, a large, dingy store in the far reaches of town, packed wall-to-wall with every imaginable cheap appliance and household good: clocks, can openers, pots and pans, eating utensils. True to its name, Francis was able to purchase a huge, clunky fan for a substantial discount. It made a shitload of noise, but when it was positioned close to his bed it did keep the room comfortably cool.

He discovered a grocery store a few blocks away from Discountland, and—risking botulism—purchased cans of food and some additional, scentless Ivory soap. The store's proprietors were a Pakistani husband and wife who seemed eager to chat, wishing him well in his new abode on Peach Street.

Francis's new roommates were Ike and Perry, both engineering students and both of them rarely on the premises. Ike was affable and surprisingly interesting. Perry was silent to the point of being almost nonverbal, but was certainly congenial enough. When Perry wasn't out somewhere, he seemed to spend most of his time holed up in his bedroom, a large bottle of vodka or Jack Daniel's at the ready. There was a girlfriend in Perry's life, Dori. Because Dori was often around, Francis was forced to interact with her on numerous occasions. She seemed like a total mismatch for the vodka-swilling engineering student, a pleasantly dull, makeup-wearing sort who seemed to have never attended college and worked full-time in some office. Dori was always very chatty and had a car of her own, a shiny candy-red monstrosity, which she would park in front of the house and which Francis could spot a block down.

It was strangely quiet here in the summer: no classes, no students; University Avenue almost entirely deserted. At times it felt like an abandoned movie set. There was something incongruous in this hot and sleepy town, with its summer heat untethered to a beach, an ocean. He had always unconsciously assumed the beach and ocean were intrinsic to summer, necessary components to the season's very existence. And yet here, with no ocean in evidence, summer—nevertheless—was in full force.

It felt as if he had the entire town to himself, availing himself of the opportunity to walk all over; not really aimlessly, but not entirely purposefully, either. He would cut across the empty commons, so dramatically devoid of students, sans that heavy, pervasive odor of food. The Feedbag became an air-conditioned refuge, Francis settling in with a stromboli and iced tea, amazed at the quiet, the lack of packed tables and frazzled staff.

In his absence, that ultra-inexpensive Chinese restaurant with the whorehouse-red interior had closed. A new, cheap Chinese restaurant had taken its place, located a block down from the old, defunct one. A makeshift used-record store—just a storefront, really—had sprung up. The Lebanese restaurant had changed its decor.

On one of his rambling walks he actually ran into someone he knew, although the name escaped him: A pleasant, preppy sort who always seemed cheerfully, perpetually overwhelmed with studying, exams, and term papers; he and Francis often commiserating in the library.

At times, during his jaunts around town, he would catch a whiff of that distinctive smell that occasionally wafted over the entire area, a smell that was instantly discernible but impossible to identify, somewhat industrial but not unpleasant in the least; an olfactory blanket that only existed here and nowhere else.

It had been a million years since he'd lived here. A million years since the dorms and Somerset Apartments. A million years since that one and only football game he'd ever attended. A million years since classes, lectures, term papers. A million years since he'd first spotted Annie on the steps of the dining hall.

The Brew 'n Wich was, to his happiness, still extant. It seemed not to have changed one grimy iota. Dough-Re-Mi too was alive and well. To his even greater surprise, its TV-trivia game was still there, perched in the very same spot, like a treasured relic. He had no interest now in this treasured relic, and in fact felt slightly uncomfortable by its very existence.

He dined at Gina's, enjoying the luxury of being practically the only customer on the premises—a table all to himself; no shortage of parmesan. Two men at a nearby booth were deep in conversation; Francis quickly determining they were faculty, bits of their scattered conversation making its way over to him; talk of sabbaticals, conferences, someone's retirement.

He took to scouring the pages of the *Dispatch* for jobs, thinking how proud Jeanette would be of him. There were also bigger, better apartment shares to be had, something to think about down the line. Perhaps he could investigate re-enrolling as well.

It didn't take long to acclimatize to the Peach Street neighborhood. A much older couple lived a few houses away; once Francis lugged a surprisingly heavy microwave up the stairs for them, earning their lasting gratitude. Russell lived across the street, an energetic, friendly sort who owned a hardware store, always cheerful and ready with a joke or comment about the weather. A loud, unpleasant gaggle of teenagers lived all the way down the block, parents rarely—if ever—in attendance. They were the only source of real noise on Peach Street, as cars were revved up from time to time, along with sporadic blasts of music and shouting.

Then there was the resident neighborhood loon, a grim-faced older man on the other end of the block, obsessed with removing every last bit of leaves, branches, and sticks from his lawn. Because one could not truly purge a lawn of all natural elements—like leaves, branches, and sticks—this was an unending task. Yet this old man kept at it, day in and day out, exploring every inch of his terrain for intrusive sticks and leaves. Francis dubbed him Sisyphus, in honor of the mythological figure who was condemned to perpetually roll a large rock up and down a hill. Ike too was familiar with the reference. From then on he and Francis began to share their steady observations: Sisyphus was out this morning; Sisyphus was lugging a particularly heavy branch; Sisyphus was mowing his lawn yet again.

37

He presented himself to a jarringly friendly temp agency and—even more jarringly—secured a steady assignment at a flowerpot company located around a half-hour away. It had never occurred to Francis that such a place as an actual flowerpot company could even exist. But exist it did, its name conjuring up images of grandiosity: JalCo Worldwide Enterprises, Inc.

It was a teeming place devoted to all things that pertained to flowerpots, helmed by the elusive Mr. Jallad, a formidable-looking man with slicked-back black hair who Francis glimpsed only on occasion. Mr. Jallad seemed always in the midst of some frenetic activity—catching a flight, attending a meeting, rushing down the hall.

Francis's own job duties were restricted to inventory and nothing but. By some logistical quirk, he managed to occupy an entire room all to himself, sitting alone at a gargantuan conference table, surrounded by overflowing piles of invoices, all of which needed to be slotted as per the five colors of JalCo flowerpots: forest green, charcoal black, mulberry purple, walnut brown, canary yellow. He existed almost entirely in his own realm, holding court behind this giant table, trying to instill some order amid the chaos of forest green, charcoal black, mulberry purple, walnut brown, canary yellow. That black indentation on his hand, now, was slowly fading.

All around him was commerce conducted on a frantic, loud basis. Who would have possibly imagined that the world of flowerpots was so involved? JalCo Worldwide Enterprises, Inc. had a huge loading dock, trucks zipping in and out. Vendors and salesmen streamed through the front office. The preferred method of communication at JalCo Worldwide Enterprises, Inc. was the intercom, which Francis could hear back and forth all day long. The loading dock seemed enmeshed in one small crisis after another. There were endless complications involving Mr. Jallad's itinerary: a limousine that didn't show up, plane tickets that never arrived.

The only real irritant was Francis's nominal supervisor, Victor, the abrasive, humorless overseer of inventory. He was from Malta, a country that Francis had always been curious about. Victor, however, was not interested in the least in discussing Malta or anything unrelated to JalCo's inventory. He communicated to Francis via a crude intercom perched in the corner of the conference room. As part of his daily routine, Francis's flowerpot reverie would be interrupted by a few unwelcome seconds of static and hiss, followed by Victor's even more unwelcome abrasive bark: "Francis! How many mulberry purple you got today?" "Francis! How many canary yellow?" The loud static, he soon discovered, gave him just enough time to bolt out of his seat and make a beeline for the men's bathroom before Victor's guttural squawk poured into the conference room. Yet Victor was more intuitive than Francis had given him credit for. He soon caught on to this not-so-ingenious ruse. "Francis! I know you hear me!" the intercom bellowed out as Francis headed for the urinals. He soon dubbed Victor the Maltese Fucker, something he shared with John, the old black janitor, who was a big Humphrey Bogart fan. "The Maltese Fucker's looking for you," he'd tell Francis. "Better get that canary yellow lined up."

Besides John, the only other bastion of calm amid JalCo Worldwide Enterprises, Inc. was the office manager, a dignified, courtly older man well into his seventies with jet-black hair. He had, he told Francis, hailed from the depths of the Ottoman Empire. As a little boy he'd gone on a lengthy family excursion in 1914, just as the First World War commenced. They were only able to return home at the war's end, four years later.

What fascinated Francis was the daily appearance of the food truck. It materialized in the parking lot around noon each and every day, complete with a clanging bell to alert the hungry. He would join the others in lining up outside for the food truck's thoroughly adequate offering of sandwiches, subs, industrial-strength coffee.

The time passed quickly. It was not, especially after working at a gas station, all that taxing. There was something unexpectedly satisfying about driving home from work at day's end and arriving home to Peach Street. Just another day at the office.

As his work assignment was drawing to an end, Francis was startled by the appearance of none other than Mr. Jallad himself, strolling into the conference room. "I'm Alex Jallad," he offered breezily, as if Francis would have no idea who he was. It had never occurred to him that Mr. Jallad even possessed a first name, much less Alex. The exotic overlay disappeared completely. Alex Jallad's accent was thick not with the Levant, but of New York City. "We're looking for sharp young people," he told Francis now. "Come talk to me when you're done with school." The implication was, of course, that Francis was now actually enrolled in college and would soon graduate. And he felt flattered that somehow Mr. Jallad himself—Alex— had picked up on his latent talents, intuiting he was a sharp young person. And Francis kicked the idea around for some time. There would be a job waiting for him upon graduation—perhaps a small office all to himself, his own intercom, learning the ins and outs of the flowerpot business. But there was no way, of course. Of that he was sure.

38.

Ike and Perry threw a bash, making the hot, cramped apartment crowded beyond belief and hotter still. They were more than gracious about including him. As it was a gathering under the aegis of two engineering students, Francis had half-expected a ploddingly dull affair, but this party was like any other he'd attended all through college. A ton of people crammed into an uncomfortable tiny space, the smell of beer permeating everything, lots of blasting music. Hours and hours later, when things had died down, it was decided to decamp to someone else's apartment a few blocks away. Francis begged off, escaping into his bedroom. When he reemerged an hour later into the deserted apartment, he was surprised to find Dori still on the premises, taking it upon herself to tidy up the kitchen. She looked hot and a little disheveled, overdressed for a college bash.

After a tentative conversational gambit of asking Francis if he was a good listener, she began a mournful, rambling discourse. Perry was irresponsible, indifferent. She had done what she could to prop up this relationship, all to no avail. He drank like a fish; everyone could see that. To Francis's increasing discomfort and fascination, Dori's tale of woe took on more intimate overtones. "I was a *good girl* before I met him," she told Francis evenly, then said it again, adding even more emphasis to the *good girl* part. This meant, obviously, she had been a virgin or simply unspoiled before she met Perry. Before he had time to process this, he heard a "Hold me" from her and then Dori—her hair, her perfume, her overdressed dishevelment—had thrust themselves into his chest. It was a disorienting onslaught. For a moment he felt alarmed. Was she offering herself to him right here and now? It turned out to be nothing of the sort. Dori merely wanted consolation and had chosen Francis as the improbable candidate. That had never happened to him before—a girl he didn't know all that well suddenly attaching herself to him, crying all the while.

Whatever differences she and Perry were grappling with were apparently unresolvable. Dori disappeared immediately after the party. That was the last Francis ever saw of her and her candy-red car.

39

In his wanderings through town he unexpectedly came across the huge deli on the corner of Essex Avenue. He stood, thunderstruck. How could he possibly have forgotten about that huge deli on the corner of Essex? When he lived in the Somerset Apartments he would come here all the time, part of his circuitous route to University Avenue, his stomach often in eagerly anticipatory knots over the prospect of running into Annie on the street or at the commons.

Now, with a growing sense of wonder, he entered. Astonishingly, it seemed to be exactly as he remembered—identical, in fact. The dispenser of black combs, each one wrapped in shiny cellophane, was positioned to the right of the cash register. The decks of playing cards were to the right of the combs. They sold everything here, an amazingly eclectic inventory of lottery tickets, cough drops, shaving cream, cans of Dinty Moore stew. The deli counter, up front, was still extant, its selection—as far as he could remember—unaltered: hunks of roast beef, salami, turkey, ham, followed by blocks of cheddar, American, and Swiss cheese. He had once, in a moment of weakness, ordered their revolting roast-beef sandwich, so greasy it dripped through the plastic wrap and paper bag and onto his newspaper, which became unreadable.

And then an even greater shock awaited him. The back corner of the deli—behind and to the right—had been perfectly, completely preserved: A stack of the *New York Times* shoved up against the wall, a stack of the *Dispatch* immediately to the right. To the right of the *Dispatch* pile was the supply of Styrofoam cups, the container of sugar packets, the milk, and box of plastic stirrers. It was as if he'd come across a portal that led into another time, place, memory.

Right here, he remembered—right on this very spot—he'd taken a Styrofoam cup, poured himself a large cup of coffee, applied sugar and milk, paid at the front, and proceeded on his way.

This was when the weather had started to turn cooler, necessitating his fall coat. He saw Annie almost as soon as he arrived on University Avenue. He'd been hoping against all hope that somehow the law of probability would work in his favor, and if he wished with enough fervor for her appearance, she would materialize right in front of him. And that was exactly what had transpired.

There was some time to spare before they each had to be at their respective classes. She accompanied him to Enoch Place. They took one of the outside benches, sitting side by side. Annie was wearing a thick green sweater, wisps of steam from her cup of coffee swirling around her hands, her face.

Autumn was just starting to make its appearance. The many trees surrounding Enoch Place were beginning to display their fall plumage of reds, yellows, browns; the first few leaves beginning to carpet the grass. The chapel, which dated from the early nineteenth century, lay across the way. And at that moment it felt as if it was just the two of them. Just the two of them, him and Annie, amid the impending autumn.

ABOUT RICHARD KLIN

Richard Klin lives in New York's Hudson Valley. He is the author of *Something to Say: Thoughts on Art and Politics in America* and *Abstract Expressionism For Beginners*. His work has been featured on NPR's *All Things Considered* and has appeared in the *Atlantic*, the *Brooklyn Rail*, the *Forward*, Akashic Books' "Thursdaze" series, and others.

www.ingramcontent.com/pod-product-compliance
Lightning Source LLC
Chambersburg PA
CBHW071938170626
46813CB00005B/1775